Once and Again

ALSO BY REBECCA SERLE

Expiration Dates
One Italian Summer
In Five Years
The Dinner List

YOUNG ADULT

Truly Madly Famously
Famous in Love
The Edge of Falling
When You Were Mine

A Novel

REBECCA SERLE

ATRIA BOOKS
New York   Amsterdam/Antwerp   London
Toronto   Sydney/Melbourne   New Delhi

ATRIA
BOOKS

An Imprint of Simon & Schuster, LLC
1230 Avenue of the Americas
New York, NY 10020

For more than 100 years, Simon & Schuster has championed authors and the stories they create. By respecting the copyright of an author's intellectual property, you enable Simon & Schuster and the author to continue publishing exceptional books for years to come. We thank you for supporting the author's copyright by purchasing an authorized edition of this book.

No amount of this book may be reproduced or stored in any format, nor may it be uploaded to any website, database, language-learning model, or other repository, retrieval, or artificial intelligence system without express permission. All rights reserved. Inquiries may be directed to Simon & Schuster, 1230 Avenue of the Americas, New York, NY 10020 or permissions@simonandschuster.com.

This book is a work of fiction. Any references to historical events, real people, or real places are used fictitiously. Other names, characters, places, and events are products of the author's imagination, and any resemblance to actual events or places or persons, living or dead, is entirely coincidental.

Copyright © 2026 by Rebecca Serle

All rights reserved, including the right to reproduce this book or portions thereof in any form whatsoever. For information, address Atria Books Subsidiary Rights Department, 1230 Avenue of the Americas, New York, NY 10020.

First Atria Books hardcover edition March 2026

ATRIA BOOKS and colophon are registered trademarks of Simon & Schuster, LLC

Simon & Schuster strongly believes in freedom of expression and stands against censorship in all its forms. For more information, visit BooksBelong.com.

For information about special discounts for bulk purchases, please contact Simon & Schuster Special Sales at 1-866-506-1949 or business@simonandschuster.com.

The Simon & Schuster Speakers Bureau can bring authors to your live event. For more information or to book an event, contact the Simon & Schuster Speakers Bureau at 1-866-248-3049 or visit our website at www.simonspeakers.com.

Interior design by Jill Putorti

Manufactured in the United States of America

1 3 5 7 9 10 8 6 4 2

Library of Congress Control Number: 2025038663

ISBN 978-1-6680-2591-8
ISBN 978-1-6680-2593-2 (ebook)

 Let's stay in touch! Scan here to get book recommendations, exclusive offers, and more delivered to your inbox.

For my father, the miracle.
And for Adele, the alchemist.

Once and Again

CHAPTER ONE

I landed, he texts me, and I feel the ground underneath my feet once again. It's 4:00 a.m. in Los Angeles, both too late and too early, but in the four years we've been together—three of them married—I've never been able to sleep while Leo is in the air.

For the past hour I've been standing in our dark kitchen, refreshing the screen of my cell phone and bathing the room in harsh blue light.

Exhale.

I pull my robe more tightly around me. I love this bungalow—built in 1958, updated in 2010; it's charming and bright. Big windows, a sliver of a garden, walking distance to Melrose Place. But there's no functional heat.

When I first moved in, six and a half years ago, the walls were green and burnt orange and the light fixtures were all brass, but over time I painted the walls white, wallpapered the bathroom, regrouted the kitchen, and decorated the space with a colorful mix of Rose Bowl Flea Market finds and Crate & Barrel sales. It's charming, and organized. Despite Leo's piles of things, I am not someone who finds clutter to be cheerful.

Go back to bed, Lauren, he writes, and I smile.

I love you.

I feel my shoulders slacken. The whirling in my stomach settles to a casual rinse cycle. He's fine.

When I was fifteen years old, my father died in a car crash. He was driving down Mulholland in the middle of a Tuesday afternoon, slightly before rush hour. He was not speeding. A teen driver in the oncoming lane was on his cell phone. Both drivers died on impact.

I flip on the electric kettle and scoop some dark roast into the pot before my eye settles on the mail stacked on our counter. Leo forgot to go through it before he left. I fan out the letters. Insurance forms for Leo, some Ralphs coupons, and a thank-you note from my friend Delia for her baby shower. We got her a bottle warmer. I run my hand over the embossed stork and then deposit the paper into the trash can.

Leo is traveling to interview for a new job. He's a DP, or director of photography. He started as a lamp operator on film sets and then got his (small) break when his old mentor from college asked him to be DP on an indie project last summer. He loved it. Today he's flying out to meet Grayson Baldacci, the wildly prolific television writer, about his new show, *Big Guys,* an office drama that will shoot in New York. If Leo gets this, it'll change the game for him. A steady gig, a regular income.

I've been an accountant for the past decade, and before that I did bookkeeping for individual clients, one of whom I still help on the side. I work at a small firm with only two other CPAs. We mostly handle retired clients living on a fixed income. The work isn't particularly glamorous, but I enjoy the steadiness of it, the reliability. And I like the business of helping people budget their lives. The obvious: It gives me great pleasure to avoid catastrophe both personally, and professionally, even if professionally I'm not following my passion.

Leo is another story. He lights up when he talks about film. Whenever we watch a movie together, he wants to run me through the cinematographer's shot list—why they chose a crane there or a wide here. I zone out, mostly, but I love how he sees the world: like a canvas waiting to be painted or captured or *told*. In Leo's universe, it's all already there; he just needs the right lens.

Water in hand, I walk over to the couch. The sunset image hanging behind it was painted by my grandmother Sylvia. It's the view at our house in Malibu—the same one I grew up in.

Did he land?

My mother. We share the same history.

Yes.

Go back to sleep.

I imagine her right now, in her frayed Ralph Lauren robe, looking out at the silver water. She isn't an early riser, my mom. That was always Dad.

My cat, Pea, stretches into the room. She looks at me wearily—*This again?*—and then abruptly leaves. She showed up on my doorstep four years ago, half a day before the biggest rainstorm Los Angeles had ever seen. I found her scratching at the glass. She was barely six weeks old, had all kinds of health issues, and no tag.

I'd never had an animal before, I wasn't even sure if I should let her inside, but Leo insisted. "The rain will kill her, Lauren," he said. "We're bringing her in."

She explored every nook and cranny of our bungalow and then promptly fell asleep on the rug. I knew before I went to bed that night that she was ours.

I start to smell the beans, and look down to see my cell phone vibrating on the counter. Leo is calling.

"You're not sleeping," he says.

I can always tell what kind of mood he's in by his voice. Leo is gregarious by nature—far more social than I am—but when it comes to our relationship, he's soft-spoken and gentle. Right now he seems chipper. But then again, it's almost 8:00 a.m. where he is. I imagine him rolling off the flight in his sweatpants and black T-shirt, his backpack on his back, duffel in hand, a hoodie slung over his shoulder. Some bagel dust down his front. He'll have slept, too. Leo can sleep anywhere.

"You're the one calling," I say.

Truth be told, I'm surprised. Leo is never on his phone. At home, that makes him a great husband—super present, rarely distracted. But when he's gone, he's often hard to get ahold of. When we first started dating I was convinced he wasn't interested because I wouldn't hear from him for days, sometimes weeks. Then he'd resurface, pick me up at my house, and look at me in a way that let me know he never forgot.

"True. Guess what? The guy next to me had never been on a plane before."

"Really?"

"Makes you marvel at the miracle of modern travel. I felt like a child again."

The coffeepot sputters and gurgles its final stream.

"How was your night?" he asks me.

I didn't sleep much—tracking his flight, watching for any type of storm warning—but I don't want to tell him that. Leo knows me, but he also knows what I tell him. We have been married only three years. There are still things to learn.

"I ordered from Pizzana with Tracy. She left around eleven. Then I did a little work."

"What did you get?"

"The white pizza. And that chopped salad with the mushrooms."

Leo hates mushrooms.

"Just remember, if you watch *Summer House* without me, I'll get an alert."

"Not if I stream it from my phone."

He lowers his voice to a growl. "You wouldn't dare."

Leo and I met at the Beach Cove, a private members-only club known for its outdated furniture and WASP culture. Neither one of us belonged—Leo insists they still don't admit Jewish people—but we were both there for Fourth of July fireworks, invited by two separate people—my friend Tracy and his friend Luke.

The thing I remember about Leo was how out of place he looked. He was dressed in sweatpants and a T-shirt, an eyeline grabber among the belted shorts and popped polos. I was surprised they let him in. And I also remember that I was attracted to him immediately. His towering frame (six foot four and two hundred and sixty pounds). His jet-black hair. And his slight English accent. He was born in Boston, raised until ten in London, and then went to boarding school in West Virginia. He's a nomad, comfortable on the road. And though he's seven years older than me, there's something so playful about him you'd swear he was younger. He also looks it.

Pea sneezes in the other room.

"I miss you," I say.

"Already?"

I take down a mug from the cabinet and pour a cup of coffee. I like it extra hot and black. I hold it between my palms. Outside I see a small bit of light start to creep through the night sky.

"I like it better when you're here."

Leo's tone softens. "I know, baby. Me, too." He clears his throat. "What time is the clinic?"

"Nine," I say. I don't want to tell him about how I needed to go in yesterday, because they weren't sure of my progesterone levels.

Leo and I have been trying to have a baby since before we were married. We knew we wanted a family, and wanted one together, and after we got serious we started trying right away. Two fertility clinics and two years later we learned the reason it wasn't happening: premature ovarian failure, which is a fancy way of saying my fertility is about the same as someone a decade older. We started to see Dr. Frankel at Reproductive Los Angeles after we got bad news at California Reproductive Center, hoping that maybe another doctor would give us better news. But we've done six IUIs and four egg retrievals, and we've never ended up with a single embryo, and I've never been pregnant. This month we did another Hail Mary IUI, just because.

"OK. Keep me posted," he says. I can hear the slight wilt in his voice, the way it flattens out whenever we talk about this.

Leo is as supportive as he can be, but fertility is a language he does not speak. No matter how many times we hear the terms *low ovarian reserve, high FSH, low AMH*, they are just obscure data points to him. They aren't real, not exactly. Not the way they are to me.

And he's tired, I know he is. "How much more of this are we supposed to put ourselves through?" He keeps asking me.

I don't know how to tell him that for me there is no answer. For me the answer is still *As much as it takes to get our baby.*

"I will," I say. I want to change the subject. "And then I thought maybe I'd go out to the beach tonight."

I can hear Leo's smile through the phone. "They'll love that."

Just then I hear a rapping at the door. I startle and some coffee spills. I took over and see him waving through the glass.

"Jesus," I say.

"What?"

"Guess."

I lift my hand to wave and mime that I'm coming to open the door, but he's already pulling out his keys.

"It's not even five a.m.!" Leo says. "OK, I'll let you go. I love you. Tell your dad he was wrong about the Lakers, and I owe him."

CHAPTER TWO

My father died in a car accident when I was fifteen, but I don't remember it, because my mother undid it. She was forty-seven when she used her silver ticket. The holy grail of gifts. All the women in my family get one, a single do-over. A chance to go back and make a different choice, unfurl a coil.

My great-grandmother was seven, or so the story goes. I never knew her. She died when I was just two years old. But the way I heard it, all those years ago, felt like a fable. Her parents were poor, and her father worked as a cobbler in Odessa. The Jewish population in 1920s Ukraine was rapidly declining. Our family had missed out on much of the wealth and stability the community had enjoyed prior to the anti-Jewish pogroms that accompanied the Russian Civil War. Some families fled to other regions, but there were rumors of attacks all over the country—nowhere was safe. There was instability and violence everywhere—but Odessa remained a center of artistic expression. It wasn't safe to be a practicing Jew, and yet, there were so many still there.

My great-grandmother was a good student, and a quick study, and she started working in her father's shop when she was just five years old. Her mother suffered from migraines and was bedridden most of the time, and so Irina would do the deliveries for her father. They were always late at night, as it was the safest time to be out, and being small—and young—she could slip by unnoticed. She'd been taught to hide and could conceal herself behind nearly anything, if need be.

One night she was out bringing a pair of shoes to the neighborhood curmudgeon—a woman named Hinda who lived just on the outskirts of town. Hinda was mean to children, scowled at her neighbors, and rarely left the house. It was rumored that her body was dotted in boils and her hair was made of snakes. She covered her hair—as many observant Jews did—so no one could be sure. Nevertheless, Irina's father gave strict instructions: "Hinda is a paying customer, and she is to be treated with respect and kindness."

Irina knocked at the door softly. No answer. Then she rapped a little harder. Still no answer. Finally she called out: "Mrs. Hinda?" She clapped her hand over her mouth, worried she had drawn too much attention to herself, but then she heard a shuffling behind the door.

There stood Hinda. Her face was knotted and gnarled; her hands gripped a small cane. She could have been sixty or one hundred and forty-eight. They seem about the same when you're seven years old.

"What?" she spat.

"I've come to deliver your shoes."

Irina held them up in their paper satchel. They were brown, drabby, Irina thought, but she said nothing of the sort. They were shoes just fine.

Hinda looked at the parcel, then at the small girl.

"I have no money for you," she said.

Irina furrowed her brow, unsure of how to proceed. Her father was clear that she must collect payment on all her deliveries. But he was also known to keep a ledger of what people owed him. "People need their shoes," he'd say. Simple as that.

Irina looked down at Hinda's feet. They were bare.

"Here you go," she said, and held the package out to Hinda. She believed it's what her father would have done.

Hinda extended her hands, unsure, tentatively receiving the shoes. She looked at Irina curiously. Perhaps no one had ever been kind to her before. Or at least not in a very many years. Maybe in a whole century.

And slowly Hinda's face began to change from suspicious to curious and then—illuminated.

"Hang on there, little girl," she said. "I do have something for you."

Hinda disappeared for what felt like a long time. It was cold, and Irina wasn't wearing a coat. She hugged her arms around her middle and waited.

Finally, Hinda returned with a small wooden box.

"Open it," she instructed Irina.

Irina opened the box. Inside was a silver ticket. It was small, about an inch by an inch.

"What is this?" Irina asked.

"It's for you," Hinda said. "In exchange for my shoes."

Hinda smiled. It was a gruesome sight. Her teeth were mangled and rotted. Irina wished she'd close her mouth.

"It is a special ticket."

"What for?"

Irina was feeling tired now, and impatient. She longed to be home with her father, for a piece of bread and a warm bed.

Hinda laughed. It was an eerie laugh, and it made Irina shiver.

"Undoing the past," she said.

And then she slammed the door in Irina's face.

Irina looked at the small wooden box, then cracked it open to check the silver ticket inside. *Undoing the past.* What did that mean? And how would Irina ever find out?

She went home hanging her head. She had no money in her pocket, which meant her mother would not get the plums she loved from the market the next day. Her father would not be able to buy meat from the butcher or more leather for the next week's repairs. She practiced what she would say, how she would tell them.

When she arrived home her father was in his shop. "How was Mrs. Hinda?" he asked.

"She could not pay," Irina said. She was next to tears.

"Did you give her the shoes?"

Irina nodded. Her father smiled.

"Good," he said. "People need their shoes."

"She gave me this."

Irina thrust the box at him. He opened it.

"My," he said. "She really must be fond of you. Next time we go, we'll bring her some apple cake."

Her father hugged her and sent her off to bed. All through the night Irina held that box. She held it pressed between her palms, and even when her eyes finally drifted closed, her fingers did not break their grasp.

The next morning she came downstairs to find her mother rocking at the kitchen table. Her father was gone. Taken. Their worst fear realized.

Irina crept into her father's shop to see it completely turned over, robbed of anything of value, most especially, its keeper. She felt a pulling in her chest. She was young enough to believe in magic but old enough to have experienced the realities of war. You could only be so young in eastern Europe. She knew if her father was gone now, he would never return.

She left her mother and climbed the stairs. She opened the box. Once again, she pressed the silver ticket between her two palms.

There is something about being a child that makes it easier to believe—and that is what happened. She thought of a time before. She thought of the previous day. She thought of her father's dirty apron and oiled hair and thick beard. She thought of his blackened fingers and long, toothy smile.

And that is how she used it, this gift from Hinda that was now more valuable than any payment could have been. She turned them back to the day before, to when he was still there.

That same night, on Irina's guidance, their family hid in the small attic above Irina's room. The shop was looted but nothing of value was taken—because nothing of value was there. The ticket was a miracle. Her father's belief in her, the second silver dollar.

"You saved us," her father would tell her. "You brilliant, blessed child."

Irina kept the wooden box, now empty of the ticket that had come in it, in that attic room that had saved her. She took it with her when she came to America, too. Afterward the ticket reappeared in the wooden box with each woman born. There was a new one when my grandmother wailed and stretched in Irina's arms, and another when my mother came in the middle of the first California snowstorm in thirty-five years. And then mine. Tucked in the safe at 31382 Broad Beach Road. Never touched.

I knew from a young age I had this ticket. And I also knew that things I could never imagine now would come into my life, and it was my job to decide which of them all was worthy of taking back.

CHAPTER THREE

I open the door, and my dad barrels inside. "I need to charge the car. Did you guys ever install that EV line?"

"Dad, it's pitch-black out."

He shrugs and then looks at me. "I knew you'd be up."

My dad and I have always been insomniacs. I think I've clocked more hours with him than any other human being. For us, 3:00 a.m. might as well be noon. When I was a teenager I would wander downstairs to find him pouring cereal or buttering toast. We'd play Rummikub or read. Sometimes we wouldn't even talk, we'd just orbit each other.

Dad empties his pockets on the counter—tissues, wallet, keys, a pack of mints, and then gets down a mug and helps himself to the coffeepot. He's not a tall man, used to be five foot nine on a good day and is now probably hovering just above five seven, his curly black hair topping the last half inch.

"There's oat in the fridge," I say.

He gave up dairy over two decades ago at the recommendation of his cardiologist. I keep some around for his spontaneous stop-bys, to ensure he has what he needs.

"Might even steam it up," he says.

"Live large," I tell him, and plug in the milk frother.

Once he's finished we take our mugs to the couch and settle against the folds of our white cotton Cloud. Leo hates this couch—he'd prefer modern lines and hard-backed chairs—but I love it. It makes me feel ensconced in a soft world. Nothing bad can get you when you're in the Cloud.

"Did you get in the water already?"

Dad shakes his head. "Nah, board on the rack, though. I thought maybe I'd check out Zuma on my way back if it's not too late." He pats my leg. "You should have seen the moon on the drive over. Ooo-weeee."

My mother hates that I live in West Hollywood. She doesn't understand why we don't move to Malibu, or, OK, Santa Monica, or even Venice, for God's sake. But I grew up on the ocean. I know it so well, its pace and rhythm all its own. It's familiar to me in ways that are both comforting—and painful. It's better for me, now, to keep my distance.

Plus, Westside home prices are even worse than West Hollywood. Leo and I could never afford it.

Dad loves it here at my house. "My pied-à-terre in the city," he calls it.

"Are you still carrying the board down yourself?"

He waves me off. "There's always someone around." He surveys the house. "How long is Leo gone for?"

"Dad," I say, ignoring the last part. "You're getting older, It's OK to ask for help. You've been there for all of them."

He raises his eyebrows at me in this way that says, *Move on*.

Dad taught me to surf when I was just four years old—tossed me on the board and paddled out, no excuses. He taught me how to head into a wave—"Paddle, don't scream"—how to dive under so as not to be knocked down, and how to time the perfect turnaround.

The ocean is a woman, baby. Never turn your back on her.

I caught my first wave alone at six, and by eight I was towing my board out myself, Dad waving from the shore.

I haven't been out in years, though. I got into the water less and less after graduation. I'm out of practice. Dad is the one who has kept it alive, kept it a part of his life.

"He's just gone until tomorrow," I say. "It's a quick trip."

He blows on the rim of his cup. Some oat foam settles on his upper lip. "How is work going for him?"

I know my dad worries about us. Will we have enough money? Will Leo "make it"? Our mortgage payments are low and our life is simple—as simple as any life can be in Los Angeles—but infertility is expensive, and the longer it goes on, the more expensive it gets. We're tapped out. There's nothing left in savings. I won't let us overextend our credit cards, not after I've seen the messes some clients have gotten into, but it means the budget is razor-thin right now. Even this six-hundred-dollar IUI meant scraping the barrel for the utility bills.

"Good," I say. "He's meeting with a showrunner this weekend. Fingers crossed." I hold mine up, locked together.

Dad beams. "They'll love him. Everyone loves Leo."

It's true; everyone loves Leo. He's warm and present, and his stature makes him look like a teddy bear. Everyone always wants a hug. When we first met I thought it was strange how many of his ex-girlfriends remained in his life—how many called on him—but as I got to know him I understood it completely. He hates letting people down, and nothing is a big deal to him. He'll drive three hours out of his way for a great scoop of ice cream, or make a run to Home Depot before they close for a pair of batteries or a pint of paint. I've never seen the man frustrated or inconvenienced in four and a half years. Except at the clinic.

But my dad—my dad especially adores Leo. His love for my husband is probably the single greatest thing in my life. Both Leo and Dad are social, but it comes out in very different ways. Leo makes people open up, and Dad opens up to people. My mom always says she'd never take a cruise with him because she wouldn't be able to walk five feet without a conversation with a stranger. Malibu is a small town—and everyone knows Dad. The barista at the Starbucks in Cross Creek, the girl who works the register at Sun Life, the waiters at Lucky's. And they all know the details of his life, too—and mine. When I got into USC our mailman left me a note that read: "Fight On."

Dad's world is full of connectivity, and when I was younger I'd always marvel at that, the way so many people cared about him. He has a bad memory—always has—and he could not be relied on to remember a birthday or a doctor's appointment—but you always got the sense when you were with him that there was absolutely nowhere else he wanted to be. He's never once looked over someone's shoulder to see who else is in the room. And he'd tell you his bank account balance over coffee.

The thing Leo and my father don't share, though, is a love of the water. Leo claims the ocean is just not his thing—he's more comfortable on land—and I used to tease him that he didn't know how to swim. The more time that has gone on, the more I think it might not be a joke. Once, on a trip to Hawaii, he walked around in the shallow end until I made him hold my hands. He lifted his legs, shook his head, and then promptly got out of the pool.

The water used to be so much a part of my life that sometimes it seems wild that my husband doesn't share my passion. That he never knew me that way. But part of adult partnership is accepting that they will never really know our before. What's important is that Leo knows who I am now, and who I will be.

"And how about you?" Dad asks. "What's new on the numbers front?"

"Reliable," I say, and he laughs.

"Better than the alternative."

Dad is a family lawyer, has been his whole life.

"I would agree."

He takes another sip, considers it. "Should we go to Urth and get oatmeal?"

Urth Caffé on Melrose Avenue is my dad's favorite haunt. It's a California café within walking distance with a big menu and decent food.

"It's not my favorite," I always tell him.

"It doesn't have to be, but it does the trick."

I look at the clock on the stove. "They don't open for another two hours."

"I'm starving. It's been three hours since I ate." He winks at me. I start to move off the couch. "I'll make you some oatmeal."

My dad sets his mug down on the coffee table. "Don't trouble yourself," he says, but he's already taking off his shoes.

CHAPTER FOUR

I started cooking sometime in the pandemic, when my main source of nutrients was frozen-food packages and then produce boxes from Jon & Vinny's, an Italian restaurant on Fairfax that became a grocer during those early months. Every week a woman named Miranda in purple plastic gloves and a paisley-print face mask would load into my back seat a box filled with beet greens, radishes, once a yellow cucumber—whatever the farmers had harvested that week—and I'd google what to do with them.

The kitchen is a stone's throw from the couch, but Dad still comes over to the counter to sit closer to me. He peels open the newspaper as I take out a pot, organic rolled oats, cinnamon, and some wild blueberries from the freezer.

Pea cozies up to the doorframe to see who is here and then backs out as quietly as she came in. She doesn't love visitors.

"I love when you cook for me," he says. "Yes, Chef!"

"It's just oatmeal."

Dad looks up at me. "You're my daughter," he says. "Everything you do impresses me."

Dad has always been effusive with his love. He'll tell me "I love you" twelve times a day. I both revel in it and at times find it challenging. Not the love or praise, but the insistence on it. The need to make every moment have some kind of meaning. I don't get these kind of displays from my mom. She's practical and careful but not necessarily warm. All the liquid in our family comes from my father.

I'm also not particularly impressive. Except, I would say, in my ability to take care of him. My mother and I have always looked after dad. Since that car accident we've stood around him like security guards—warding off any possible danger.

My mother wishes he would stop surfing—it's dangerous and physical, that's for certain. I worry about it less than she does, though. Maybe because for so many years I was out there with him.

"You need to relax a little about your dad," Leo will tell me. "He's good! Let the man live." But Leo also doesn't know. He doesn't know about the accident, or the remaining silver ticket that sits locked away in Malibu. It is not his secret, it's ours.

The water boils, and I drop the oats in, turning the temperature down to a simmer. Dad likes thick oatmeal, so do I, and I wait until it starts to pop and bubble before adding in raisins and blueberries and giving it a good stir.

I load the contents into bowls, heap cinnamon and maple syrup on top—plus a little Trader Joe's granola for crunch—and pass one to him. Steam rises off the top in aromatic waves. Dad takes his glasses off to eat.

"Oh, wow," he says. "This is delicious. You do it better than Urth, that's for sure."

I join him at the counter as the sun creeps farther across the floor, like a teenager trying to sneak in unnoticed.

We eat in silence for a few moments.

"So what's on the docket for today?" he asks.

"A few meetings," I say. I take a lot of them virtually from home these days. "Probably leftovers for lunch. And then I thought I'd spend the night at the beach."

Dad's eyes twinkle. "We'd love that," he says. "Shabbat pasta."

Sylvia's Friday night special. Sometimes I wonder how my dad feels about still living with his mother-in-law all these years later. I've never asked him. I'm sure if I did he'd say "You know I love her," or "Sylvia is Sylvia!" There are few situations Dad doesn't find the good in. He's broken his leg, dealt with disease, lost both of his parents, and abandoned the hope of having a tool shed. He's never lost his smile.

It wasn't until two months after Dad's accident that my mother and grandmother told me about the tickets. Right after it happened my mother fell into a depression. She'd sit at home . . . inside, never out, never on the beach—too much air, breath, *movement*— and stare at the television. No one knew anything had occurred, so no one knew what was wrong. No one except Sylvia.

"Something has happened," my grandmother told me, although she didn't say what, or to whom.

It was only when I found my mom in the shower, slumped over, skin rubbed raw, that I demanded an answer. Marcella had always been a little nervous, yes, but never catatonic, never absent, never *this*.

"What happened?" I asked her. "What is happening?"

They sat me down in my bedroom, Marcella and Sylvia. I remember because there was a Kelly Slater poster on the wall that still hangs there, peeled and yellowed at the edges—that I can't look at without remembering that day. The one when my whole world changed.

"She's too young," my grandmother said. She'd been saying it since I'd found Marcella, since she'd come up the stairs, since she'd forced Sylvia to sit down on my bed.

"She needs to know what she has," my mom said.

Sylvia shook her head. "It's not the right decision."

"You don't know what the right decision is." My mother turned on her. Marcella was sullen sometimes, but I rarely saw her angry, never heard her raise her voice. She wasn't that kind of mother. You knew her anger in her silence.

"Please," I said, both to get them to stop and to get them to just say it.

Sylvia looked at me. I saw her head imperceptibly nod.

She came toward me and took my hands in hers. Sylvia's hands were always cold, but that day they didn't feel like cool, familiar relief—they felt like shock.

"We're different," Marcella said, and Sylvia's grip on my hand's tightened. "We have something other people don't."

My mother pinched the bridge of her nose with her thumb and forefinger. I could see her physically deflating.

"Go ahead, then," Sylvia said, and I thought it was the most unattractive she had ever looked.

I remember thinking I didn't recognize her. That someone else was in the room with us.

"Sweetheart," my mom said, her tone changing. "Do you know how lucky you are?"

I felt the hairs on the back of my neck stand up. I did know I was lucky. I knew in all the ways they tell you to be grateful. Two parents, enough food, good health. My hair was frizzy, but so what, right? Most of the time it was wet anyway. I was lucky for my proximity to the water, that I could admit. How did people grow up in big, wide swathes of dry land? I knew that my parents, even then, were far more concerned with each other than with me. But I had an eerie sense that was not what she meant. I all at once was not sure I wanted to know what came next.

"I don't know," I said.

Sylvia smiled. And then she laughed. A big, wholehearted laugh. I loved her laugh. Every time she laughed I felt it was in delight—at life, and sometimes, in some precious moments, at me. But this laugh was different. It was maniacal. This laugh was not in excess of joy but in reaction to inevitability, to ridiculousness, to the unimaginable reality that this was her life, her family, this moment.

She set a hand on my cheek. It was still cold.

"You get a do-over," Sylvia told me. Simple, brief, clean.

I felt the air slice with her words. Next to me, Marcella exhaled.

I asked the only thing I could think to. I was pretty sure, after all, that I understood the answer. "For what?"

"Something happened recently," my mother said.

"Use the real words," Sylvia said. Her voice was powerful, defiant. She spoke as if she were holding Marcella to the fire. She opened her mouth again, to say what came next, and Marcella leaped in.

"She's my child," she said simply.

My mother looked at me. I could see how red her eyes were—she looked like she hadn't slept in days. There was intention in them when she spoke. When I look back on her words, the way they transformed, it appears almost cruel, the way she said what she did next.

"Your father died in a car accident," Marcella said. She didn't hover. She didn't trip over the words. Out they came. "But I took it back, and now he's here. And now here we are."

Sylvia looked at my mother with a mix of pity and what I thought might have been regret. It looked like maybe she was going to hug her, or at the very least set a hand on her shoulder, but she didn't.

I felt my heart rate quicken. I had no idea what they meant, but also, strangely, I did. I knew in the way you know when things are true.

Truth is easy to understand, even when it is unbelievable.

"That's why you've been depressed," I said.

My mother looked to my grandmother, who nodded.

"Anything that happens, that you want to undo, you get to," Sylvia said. "One time."

I could think of plenty of things to undo. I had forgotten to use deodorant during track practice last week. I'd brought an egg salad sandwich to school—big mistake. I'd told Carlie that Phil wanted to go out—that one backfired.

But I understood that was not what they meant, that was not what I was being told. My mother had just saved my father's life.

I looked at Marcella. She started to cry. I felt her grief move out of her and into me like a kind of virus, infecting everything in spit distance. I understood her grief and pain and terror—because somehow it was mine, too. I could see that it connected us and *would* connect us from now on.

When I look back and think about the moment I became an adult, it was not the following year, when I lost my virginity, or going to college, or my first job or paycheck or any of the markers people use to denote the passage of time. It was this.

What is adulthood if not the recognition of responsibility?

We left that bedroom three women, tethered, however reluctantly, by our one, singular fate.

My mother recovered, slowly, but she was never quite the same. And I held on to that, what it meant, what she was, without words, telling me. Everything awful is on the other side of that ticket. Because on the other side of that ticket you had no more cards to play. On the other side of that ticket was just the relentless, mercilessness of life.

From that point on we were different, but we were also united in this dance around my father, this drive to protect him.

Dad and I finish our oatmeal, and he does the dishes, stacking them neatly on the drying rack before smacking his hands together.

"OK, babycakes, I'm out of here. Going to see about some waves."

I make a face, somewhere between joy and concern, and my father rolls his eyes. "I'm always careful," he says. "You don't even have to say it."

But I do anyway. This is my story.

CHAPTER FIVE

Her story starts further back, but not that much further, in the grand scheme of things. Marcella Steiner never changed her name, not that it matters. Everyone still calls her Marcella Novak, or honey, or, more to the point, *Mom*. But this is not a story about a woman put upon by motherhood—at least, no more so than any story about a mother is about a woman who is put upon by motherhood. Marcella likes having a house that is her own and a family that is her own. It gives her a sense of peace and purpose in a disjointed and surprisingly barbaric world.

She got married when she was twenty-four, an age her mother thought ridiculous but society deemed accomplished. It was the eighties. She was bathed in attention and warmth and praise. How wonderful to have met a lawyer! How wonderful to be living in her childhood home as a young bride! Marcella reveled in this rightness. Finally, finally, she felt she was where she belonged.

She got married not at the beach but inside Sinai on Wilshire, the same temple to which she has belonged the entirety of her marriage, even though her husband and daughter do not find conservative Judaism as rewarding as she does (once they called it "conformist," she stopped asking them to come to services with her). This bothers her more than she'd admit, but her rabbi tells her that faith cannot be forced, and for the most part, she agrees.

She wore a cream, not white (a more flattering hue, Sylvia told her) dress to her ankles and a veil that covered her face. Afterward there was a reception in the banquet hall with sparkling wine and bagels and lox. The wedding was called for 11:00 a.m. By 2:00 p.m. they had consummated the marriage and her husband was out on the water, where he has remained for many of the past thirty-nine years.

She loves her husband. David is a good man and a kind father and a great partner, and she knows how rare it is to find all three. He calls to ask if there's anything she needs him to pick up on his way home from work, and he puts his shoes away from the door, and he makes sure sex is fulfilling. She does not mean to make their marriage seem robotic, convenient, or even equitable; it is none of those things. Dave never remembers to close doors or put away socks or make doctor's appointments. He'd never prepared a meal for himself, not even toast. Marcella's marriage is remarkable and unfair, as many marriages are.

Today Marcella is in an argument with Sylvia—the same one she has had countless times before. Marcella does not know why Sylvia insists on leaving the gate open at night, or forgetting to lock it, as the case may be. Her mother is nearing ninety-two, but that is no excuse, because her memory fails her nowhere else but this one, singular thing. Their safety.

"You're so uptight," Sylvia tells her, a familiar refrain. It frustrates Marcella—that she has been cast as the tightly wound coil to Sylvia's free-flowing silk. It isn't fair that women are chastised for freedom while young and condemned for order later.

"I just want to make sure no criminals come up off the beach and into our home while we are sleeping," Marcella says. "Is that really too much to ask?"

"When has that happened even once in the decades we've lived here?" Sylvia says.

It only takes one, Marcella thinks, and she knows her mother can sense the words, even if she doesn't say them out loud.

Sometimes Marcella wonders how she would have turned out if she had had a mother who loved rules. Would she have been a free spirit? Worn long dresses? Traded her name into Sanskrit? If she hadn't had to keep the rails on, might her daughter see her differently? Might she see her as someone sparkly, too? Someone who she'd want to drink wine at night with and tell her secrets to? Lauren has always been closer to Sylvia than she is to Marcella.

Are we all just the antithesis of where we come from?

The phone rings, startling her away from this repetitive argument. Lauren is calling.

"Hi, Laur."

Marcella picks up on the first ring, aware that this seems slightly desperate, and then annoyed that she is able to clock such things, that she still wants to seem cool and busy to her daughter—is still trying to convince Lauren that she has her own life, her own priorities. Anything that might remind her daughter that she is more than her mother and Dave's wife.

"I'm going to come out tonight," Lauren says.

She doesn't ask, which bothers Marcella, but not for the reasons you'd think. It bothers her because she sees the house as the ocean, not as home, and Marcella wants her to feel this is her home, still. To not just visit Broad Beach for the waves—a weekend, stay over and surf on Saturday—but for her, for their family.

"Great," Marcella says. "Sylvia is cooking."

"It's Friday," Lauren says, when she might as well say, *Obviously*.

Marcella can hear Lauren rattling around with some papers and assumes she is busy, so she pretends she is. "I have to run. I'm setting up for cards."

"Have fun. See you later."

In another moment, silence.

Her card game hasn't met in almost two months because Cindy Miller got Covid and then no one wanted to get together, even after the five days had passed, and then schedules were conflicting, and now she wonders if she has a weekly game at all.

The front door opens, and Dave comes through.

"Sweetheart," he says. "How about some breakfast?"

It's past nine in the morning, and she knows he has been up for hours. She assumes he went surfing, and then to coffee, because that's his usual, although sometimes it's the other way around. She does not think about the possibility that he has been to Lauren's, that they have shared their version of family before Marcella even awakens.

"Sure!" she says. She goes upstairs to get her sun hat. When she comes back down he's asleep on the couch. She covers him with a blanket, noting the oatmeal stain on his shirt.

CHAPTER SIX

The drive to Broad Beach down the Pacific Coast Highway is one of my favorite stretches of land in the world. Not that I've seen them all, or even that many in my thirty-seven years. I've been to Europe once, never South America or Africa—or even Morocco. There were a few trips to Hawaii, and one to Mexico, both over a decade ago. I used to travel with my parents, but lately they don't get on planes as much, and neither do I. There was never a huge need to leave, either. Malibu has the ocean—and I was happy to spend whatever vacations we got in the water.

Today it's still bright sun as I make my way out, and the salt air hits as soon as I turn off Entrada and onto the highway. Even in traffic the sea breeze is clear. You don't have to be moving fast to feel it. It's just there. It'll greet you at a standstill.

It's this landscape that I love. The familiar bend of the road, the way as soon as the ocean comes into view I feel like I could drive with my eyes closed. There's a downshift that happens on this drive, the drive home.

I leave Pea home when I come to the beach. We put out extra food, and the neighbor comes and checks on her—the one stranger she actually seems to like. So it's just me in the car.

I pass Dad's office, the same place he has worked since the eighties, and then Cross Creek—the country mart with all the high-end shopping centers and restaurants. On my left a little way up is the Colony—an exclusive enclave of Malibu complete with a gated community and at least four A-list movie stars. And then Pepperdine University up past the hill.

I take the highway farther, past Geoffrey's, to where the land starts to split. I pass Paradise Cove and Point Dume and then I turn off Pacific Coast Highway at Broad Beach and take the road all the way down.

31382 Broad Beach greets you shyly. The house doesn't look like much from the car—an old, shingled, crumpling pile of wood—but once you're through the driveway and up to the front door, you start to get a sense of her splendor. It has peeling paint, a roof that is flat in places and angled in others, out-of-style bay windows, and a wood door stained with sun spots. But none of that matters because the house is right on the ocean.

The house is old, but that's less of an anomaly in Broad Beach than it is in other spots in Malibu. Still, we are surrounded by mega mansions and multimillion-dollar renovations. My parents have never really touched the place. For one, they never could have afforded it, construction costs being what they are, but for another, they love this house—we all do. It's like a living piece of history, our history. They've done small things—repainted and regrouted—but the windows are the same bays from the eighties, there's pottery painted red with turquoise on the inside, and the granite in the bathroom is a pink geometric shape running up and down the walls. The house leaks when it rains and heats up to ninety-three degrees in the summer when the glass windows magnify whatever light is outside. But to me, it's perfect.

They could sell it for millions, it's true, but every time someone knocks on the door with an offer—and they do often—Sylvia always gives them the same answer: *I'm not going anywhere.*

The house sits directly on Broad Beach—a public beach and a great surf spot. The plot of land is also the largest on the strip, so while the house is modest, there is space for a small back cottage—a bedroom, bathroom, and kitchenette—where most of the houses are mere feet apart. This is where Sylvia lives now. It has easy access to the garden and is all one level.

I park behind my dad's silver Volvo station wagon, and as soon as I open my door, I'm immediately struck by the ocean air. It's heady, dense, mixed with the florals that creep up the shingled walls.

The same roses have grown out here my whole life—hearty ones, big and pink and plump. There were two years when they didn't bloom because of the drought, and we thought maybe they were gone for good, but they came back with the rain—more Technicolor than ever before. The garden is properly weeded but grapevines crowd out passion fruit in a tangled ballet against the side of the house. There are overgrown bushes, and a pile of a fig tree that's been trying to die for the past eighteen months. There's a terra-cotta pot directly outside the door with an olive tree inside that's just beginning to fruit, and above it hang some wind chimes that are dancing in the sea breeze.

I don't knock, just open the door. It's unlocked, of course. It's always unlocked, to Marcella's dismay. But this is the beach. There's an inherent trust to the coastline houses that persists.

I'm greeted immediately with the smells of garlic and oil and herbs. I follow my nose to the back of the house, where Sylvia is in the kitchen chopping onions and sautéing sprigs of rosemary—almost certainly from the garden. She turns around when she hears me, wiping her hands on a dish towel.

"Mamashana," she says. "Let me see you."

She takes me into a hug, and I feel her bony body in my arms. She'll be ninety-two this fall, but the woman acts like she's sixty. She let her hair go gray in her forties, so I don't remember a time before it was silver—although it's shorter now than it ever used to be. Her skin bruises, so she wears long sleeves, even in the summer, and she's thinner, but she's still so quintessentially Sylvia. She still wears mala beads in heavy strands around her neck, and canvas hats nearly everywhere, even inside, and wide-legged Indian-print pants. And she's always barefoot. "The secret to a long life is to feel the ground," she always tells me.

"Hi, G-money," I say. I've been calling her that since childhood. Likely because she used to give me an extra allowance, although, like all things from memory, hard to know. "Where is everyone?"

I look around the house. A cookie jar—a butler, holding a bottle of champagne—sits proudly on the kitchen counter; I can remember it being stocked with knobby granola bars as a child. From the kitchen you can see straight back to the entry and directly out to the water. To the left of the kitchen is the living room with large, oversize paisley-print sofas, mismatched plaid and floral pillows, and an antique wood credenza. There's also a grandfather clock that stands proud in the corner and a glass hutch that displays what feels like hundreds of different dishes and glassware. Sylvia has always loved to thrift.

She gives the oil and herbs a good stir.

"Your mother went for a walk; your father's upstairs." She sets the wooden spoon she is using down. "And you are here. You want to help an old lady?"

I move to wash my hands at the sink. "I'd love to."

She hands me some eggplant to skin and chop and then points to a basket of vine-ripened tomatoes. "I thought about putting together a little salad," she says. "What do you think?"

I pull open the fridge, already searching.

"Top shelf," she says, and I pull down the burrata. We grin at each other. Exactly what I was looking for.

Sylvia always cooks with a glass of wine, and in her hand now is a glass of white, beads of sweat running down the glass.

"You want one?" she asks me.

I pull a cup out of the china cabinet—something porcelain and round—and hand it to her in answer.

The kitchen has a door that leads to a bleached-out wooden deck that hangs over the sea, with steps down to the ocean. It's still early—only five o'clock in the summer—and the sun is blazing high. The water is a stunning, sparkling blue.

"Where's Leo?" she asks me.

I pick up an eggplant and start to skin it with a knife. "New York for work. He'll be back tomorrow."

When I was growing up I'd watch my grandmother in the kitchen every day. She always fed our family. My mom was never really that interested in cooking, and Dad can't tell an orange from a spatula, so Sylvia did all the meals. Salads were from the garden, the wide array of ingredients dependent on the time of year. There'd be cucumbers in May, tomatoes in July, delicata squash and snap peas in September. Potatoes and zucchinis as the weather got cooler. When I started cooking, it felt like a language I'd once known as a child but had since forgotten.

I chop shallots, mix a tangy lemon-and-mustard-seed dressing with tarragon and olive oil. As I cook, my eye keeps being pulled out to the water. Sylvia notices.

"Why don't you go find your mom?" she says. She takes a long sip of wine. "It's early, yet. There's plenty of time." She sets her glass down. "You know Marcella. She's probably out there worrying about the tide."

"Ha," I say.

My grandmother raises an eyebrow at me. "Worry gets you nowhere." Another familiar refrain.

I laugh again. "Might be too late for that."

She puts a hand tenderly on my shoulder. "It's not ever too late," she whispers. "I just took up Pilates."

Sylvia has never told us what she used her do-over for, only that it happened a very long time ago. "Maybe a night with Kennedy," she sometimes says. "You think Marilyn was the only one who shot her shot?" Or: "I once sold this house, regretted it, now it's like it never even happened." Or: "Oh, there could have been a small plane crash. Who would remember."

The answer is always the same: *It's none of your business.*

I give Sylvia a kiss on the cheek. She smells like her Pond's cream, like she always does. The two most comforting scents in the world: the ocean and Pond's face cream.

"Don't lift the pots. They're heavy," I tell her.

She swats me away with a dish towel. "Still my kitchen. Get out!"

I follow her instructions, setting my shoes at the door and walking out onto the deck. My parents had the stairs redone about a decade ago because the sand had receded so much that the last step no longer reached the ground. It hung midair, and for a while we jumped, but as my parents got older it became less desirable—and of course Sylvia couldn't visit the sand at all, so they sprung for some new stairs.

I don't know if Sylvia comes down too often, though. It makes me sad to think about her no longer visiting the water, although she was never a big ocean swimmer. She used to take water aerobics every Wednesday at the community pool on the Malibu High campus but rarely went in the water here.

I'm careful to avoid the places with split wood as I cuff my jeans up to my calf and take the steps down to the beach. When my feet hit the sand my toes immediately sink down into the dampness. The water comes up quickly and licks at my heels. It's icy cold. Even in the summer, the ocean in California is like a freezer. You can polar-plunge all year long.

I don't see my mom in either direction, but I start walking in her favorite—to the right—because the sand runs for longer than it does to the left. The sun is directly in my eyeline, and I hold my hand up to shield my face. I should have brought a hat—Marcella is always going on about the dangers of sun damage—but the sun on my face always felt too good to waste. I close my eyes and lift my chin upward.

I left my phone at the house, and now I'm wishing I had it with me to take a picture for Leo. When we were first dating I'd bring him down to Malibu—not the house, not at first, but to Point Dume and the Sunset Restaurant at Zuma Beach. I wanted him to know the place I was from first, before the people. I wanted him to fall in love with this same coastline.

And he did. Not the beach, not exactly—the man has worn shorts only twice in his life—but the beauty. He got it immediately. Every time we come down now he brings his camera and just stands on the steps, shooting. I love that even though he doesn't understand the water, he can admire it.

I think about his voice through the crashing of the waves. *Hey, baby, hang on just a tick.* . . . I wonder what he's doing right now. Transversing the city, underground on the subway. Leo would never spring for a cab on his own dollar.

When I met Leo I had been single for a really long time. I was nearly thirty-three, an age where I sometimes thought my best relationships might have been behind me. And a point at which I had become settled in my singlehood.

I remember being worried about fitting someone into my life, how I'd have to sacrifice all the freedom I had grown accustomed to. But being with him was so easy. Every time he was at my house I wanted him to stay, and every time he was gone I missed his presence.

And then one day he was on his way over to mine and the phone rang. He'd tripped at a shoot, fallen on some heavy equipment. He told me his arm was hurt, maybe broken. My back broke into a cold sweat.

I met him at the urgent care. He was sitting on a gray plastic chair, trying to fill out the intake forms with his left hand. He looked so much younger than forty. He looked like a child.

"Here," I said, "let me do it."

I had watched my mom handle all the paperwork for my dad. I knew my way around a clipboard.

We sat in that waiting room for over an hour, his good hand on my knee and my head on his good shoulder. And I knew then I wasn't scared of losing my freedom, not anymore. I was scared of losing him. My happiness was now dependent on the safety of someone else.

I let my memory linger in those early days. When everything about our relationship felt precious and tender. How at ease I felt in my body just knowing him.

"Lauren!"

By the time I hear him, I know it isn't the first time he's called my name.

I know it before I say it, before I even turn around. I can feel it in the way my chest reacts, in the tension that shoots from my sternum down my limbs.

Stone Morrow.

He extends his hands and smiles wide. "It is you."

I take him in in fragments because it is too much to absorb him all, here all at once. Bare-chested, rash guard pulled off. Loose, long hair—longer than I remember. Dimples the size of potholes.

He comes toward me, closing the eight feet between us, and offers me a shallow hug. He's damp to the touch, and I can smell the ocean—visceral—on him. I have a flash of us, barely seventeen, bobbing on our boards at dawn. He pulls back and looks at me, holds his hand on my shoulder.

"Just came off the water," he says. "Wow, incredible. You're here."

Stone and I dated from fifteen to twenty-five, a full decade and what felt like more than a few lifetimes. We've seen each other only a handful of times in the intervening decade. His family still lives down here—we grew up as kids together, and it became something more midway through high school. For more than a decade now he's lived in Boulder, Colorado, where he started a school modeled on Kelly Slater's Surf Ranch—a man-made ocean that can simulate waves for lessons and training. I think it's successful, but I've never really looked into it. For many years it was too painful, to think about the life he had somewhere else. It also didn't make sense to me that he had to build an ocean out there when there's one right here.

"It's good to see you," I say. I hug my arms around me partly because the dampness from our hug has made me cool and partly because there's something about being around Stone—even all these years later—that makes me want to protect myself. "How long are you in town?"

He squints past me, out to the water. "Not sure, actually," he says. He takes a big breath. "Bonnie's not doing so good."

Bonnie is Stone's stepmother, but she raised him from the time he was six years old. His mother moved to Canada when he was just a toddler, and he saw her on holidays, sometimes a stretch in the summer. I always thought that must have been really hard—having your mother leave so young, but Stone never seemed to harbor any resentment toward her or what happened.

"If she'd stayed I'd never have Bonnie," he said.

From the way Bonnie tells it, the moment she met Stone's father she liked him, and the moment she met Stone she was in love.

"I'm sorry, shit. I didn't know," I say. "Marcella didn't say anything."

I wonder why my mother hasn't told me. But then I think about how little we talk on the phone these days. How she'll call and I often send it to voicemail, anticipating some kind of reserved judgment. I know I am also to blame. I don't talk about my life with her, I never really have. But the past few years the space between us has felt even more pronounced—like I finally named and saw all the distance that was always there. Part of it is that I don't talk about the fertility stuff with her. The truth is, I don't really talk about it with anyone. But there is something different about not sharing with your mother.

Stone waves a dismissive hand. "She's kept it pretty quiet." He wipes some wet hair off of his face. He's always had a face full of freckles, but they are less pronounced now than they once were. "It's been back for a while now. The last round didn't work as well. We're looking into some experimental stuff, you know. I just wanted to be close." He squints out at the horizon and then back to me.

I nod. "Of course, yeah. I'm sorry."

We stand there for a minute, suddenly aware of the awkward nature of this interaction. How much there is to say, and how little.

"So," he says. "What's new with you?"

He laughs when he says it, and so do I, because the question is ridiculous. It still feels wild, all these years later, that we do not know. That we are strangers to each other now.

"Still in West Hollywood."

Stone smiles. "Still working for Wagner?"

"Indeed."

He nods. I decide to say it, because I'm sure he already knows, even if he's not on social media, and because it feels important to say. To claim Leo's presence here.

"And I got married."

"I heard. I'm happy for you."

It's genuine, honest. If I'm hoping for a flare of jealousy, I don't get one.

It's been so long since we were anything close to romantic. Time for jeans to stop being baggy and go back to being baggy again. But there are some relationships where the origin just feels so close to the surface. No matter how much time passes, it's still there. The kinetic energy that once connected us has never transformed. Maybe because we were so young when it began.

"Hello!" I see Marcella from down the beach.

Her arms wave at us overhead. I feel irritated at the interruption, but then remember I came out here looking for her.

Stone waves back equally dramatically, matching her.

"Darling!" she says when she reaches us. She flings her hands on top of her head to hold her hat down as a big gust of wind blows by. She's wearing linen pants pushed up to her shins and an open, billowy button-down. Her straw-colored bob is tucked behind her ears, and she has a singular strand of pearls around her neck. She looks like she belongs in Amagansett or Nantucket with a trail of golden retrievers. But she lives in Malibu and is allergic to dogs.

Stone smiles. "Marcella, you look stunning."

"Oh, come here," she says. "Give me that face." She pulls him into a hug and then holds him at an arm's length. My mother has always loved Stone. "This body. You don't change."

"You knew me when I was ten," Stone says. "I hope that's not the case."

My mother waves him off. "How is Bonnie, baby? Tell me."

I feel a pang that my mom knew but didn't think to mention it to me.

Stone inhales with his mouth open. When we were together I used to stick my finger through his lips when he was thinking.

"You should come visit," he says. He doesn't say it somberly, not exactly, but we both know what he means.

My mother nods. "I will."

All at once Stone seems to become aware of his board, that the task he set out to accomplish has long since been completed. "I should head in," he says. "Great to see you both."

He gives me a small smile and then takes off down the beach. My mother comes and stands shoulder to shoulder with me as we watch him leave.

"Still gorgeous," she says.

"Why didn't you tell me about Bonnie?" I say.

I feel her inhale next to me. "I didn't want to upset you," she says.

We watch Stone pick up his board, like it's no more than a book, and head up the steps.

"He's just so strong," she says, and I know what she means.

The only person in my life I never had to worry about getting hurt.

CHAPTER SEVEN

We eat as the sun descends. Linguini with clams and garlic oil, roasted eggplant, salad with shallot vinaigrette and heirloom tomatoes with the soft burrata from the top shelf. The house has an open dining room that spills out onto the deck, and we keep the doors open throughout dinner, hearing the waves crash.

"I love this salad dressing," Marcella says.

"It's the herbs," Sylvia says, wrapping another bite on her fork. "They make the dish."

Marcella is the one who tends the herb garden out front, and I take Sylvia's comment as an out-of-character compliment—I wonder if my mother does, too. It still surprises me, sometimes, how different the three of us are. How even after all this time, even after everything we share—blood, this gift, a genetic lineage, this home—my mother and grandmother remain somewhat of a mystery to me.

"Are you going to stay the weekend?" my dad asks.

"I hadn't decided yet," I say. "Leo isn't back until tomorrow night. I left Pea enough food for it, though."

"You'll stay," Sylvia says. "Tai chi meets here tomorrow night."

"I've never seen so many people drink wine at a tai chi night," my dad says.

"It's good for the vibes," Sylvia says.

"You really shouldn't do too many one-leg balances," my mother says, and at that Sylvia changes the subject.

Afterward my parents and I clean up and Sylvia retires to her back house.

"See you in the morning," she says. "But not too early! Don't go banging on my door until it's time for a mimosa."

She's always slept late. When I was a child and she still lived upstairs, I remember I was allowed to knock on Sylvia's door only after 9:00 a.m. I'd crawl into bed with her, and we'd watch *Live with Kelly* or *The View*.

"All these women do is talk over each other," she'd say, but she watched anyway. We'd share her coffee, me sneaking sips and Sylvia pretending not to notice until the cup ran cold or it was empty.

I dry out the orange Le Creuset pot and store it under the stove. My mom has already gone up, and it's just me and Dad left in the kitchen.

"Tea or another glass?" he asks me.

I slide the bottle of cab across the table to him, and he pours for us.

"Good choice."

Without saying anything, we take our glasses outside. We settle into sun chairs on the deck, side by side. The breeze off the ocean is almost cold now. I pull over my head a stray sweatshirt that's been discarded by someone—probably Dad—earlier today.

Dad takes a sip. "I don't know if I should be flattered or worried that my thirty-seven-year-old daughter still can't spend a night alone."

I exhale out a laugh. "I can. I think. I mean, I could."

"Yes, very convincing."

Before I met Leo, spending the night alone in the bungalow was habit, routine. But since I've been with him, any time I'm alone there I start to feel like I'm on high alert. What if an intruder comes in? What if that earthquake finally hits and we can't find each other? Being tethered to someone ups the survival stakes.

"I ran into Stone today."

Dad just looks at me, raises his eyebrows slightly, waiting for me to continue.

"I guess Bonnie isn't doing so good. Mom never mentioned it."

Dad nods. "You're busy, honey," he says. "She doesn't want to bother you. You're not always easy for her to get on the phone." Then: "How was seeing him?"

I think about it. "Fine," I say. "Strange. I think the last time I saw him was five years ago."

"Before Leo."

I nod.

"He's a nice guy," Dad says carefully. "But he wasn't the one for you."

"Is that what he is?" I say. "Nice?"

Dad laughs lightly, and I feel us exhale into the space between us, the ease that has just always been there. Dad was the one who I could go to, the one who wouldn't punish me if I screwed up on an exam, or stole a vodka bottle from the liquor cabinet. Dad was always able to see the context in whatever I had done. He was never hard-lined, always inquisitive. He was the first person I told after Stone and I had sex for the very first time.

"It's better to think of old loves as nice," he says. "Keeps you out of the muck. If someone is an asshole, well—that's fire. Fire is alive, you get me?"

I do. Stone was never an asshole. But then again, nice is not how I'd describe our relationship, not exactly.

"Things work out," I say. "I'd never have Leo."

"That's right."

I look out over the water. The seafoam appears iridescent against the black sky. It feels like we are both waiting for me to say it, and so I do.

"But Stone was there, you know?"

He witnessed our history. He was there for so much of my becoming.

Dad knows about his car accident. My mother told him. I don't know how the conversation went, because I wasn't there—I just know that one day my mother and Sylvia and I had a secret, and the next all four of us did. My father, by all accounts, believed her immediately. Not just because he loves her—although I suspected that was most of it—but because, as he put it, it seemed to explain a lot about her nature, why she had become so drawn and anxious.

It connected them more deeply, deeper than they had been before. I've heard only children sometimes say that they feel a part of their parents' marriage. That there is no "us" and "them" but instead just "we." That there is no separation between a marriage and a family when there is only one child.

But I always felt like a little bit of an outsider to my parents' marriage. I suspected my dad was my mom's priority, and I didn't resent it, exactly, but I didn't like it, either. And after the accident it went from suspected to obvious. To fact. My mom orbited around him—the man she loved, the man she had saved, the man she'd do anything to protect. And so I started to protect him, too.

I hear my phone ringing, a soft hum from inside. It jolts me out of the moment.

"Go," Dad says. "I'll close up."

I kiss him on the cheek and head inside. Leo is calling.

"Baby!" he says. His voice rings through the phone loud and clear and happy. "How's it going out there?"

"Good. Dad and I are just having some wine outside. How are you?"

I toss some paisley pillows on the floor and sink down into the old leather couch.

"What did Sylvia make?" he asks.

"Pasta," I say. "Among other things."

"Shabbat spaghetti?" His voice gets farther away and then comes back again.

I hear a door slam.

"Save me some of those leftovers."

Dad turns around and waves through the glass. I wave back and mouth *Leo* to him. He gives me a thumbs-up.

"So tell me how it went," I say into the phone.

"Wait, hang on. Just gotta—"

Leo is a terrible multitasker. If I ask him a question while he's chopping an onion, I have to repeat myself three times.

I hear the front door rattle. My heart thumps, and I took toward the deck—*Where is my dad? Is this an intruder?*—but then the door swings open and there is Leo.

He has a backpack on his shoulders that he slides off as soon as he gets inside.

"You're here!"

I toss my cell on the couch and throw my arms around his neck. I feel his hands press into my back, holding me firmly to him. I breathe in his Leo scent—comforting, like an old bookstore. My heartbeat slows.

"You're here!" I say again. "Why are you here?"

Leo releases me and nods to my dad, who has just come inside. "Sorry to interrupt."

Dad pats him on the shoulder. "Not at all," he says. "Glad you're back. I'm gonna go to bed. I'll see you two tomorrow."

He kisses me on the side of my head and then carries on up the stairs, leaving us alone. I take Leo's hand and lead him down onto the couch.

"When did you leave?" I say at the same time he says: "I got the job."

I see the smile on his face—the slow spread of it. My eyes go wide.

"Babe. That's amazing." I put my hands on either side of his face. "I'm so proud of you."

He leans his forehead down to touch mine, then pulls his head back up.

"So, listen," he says. He takes my hands off his face and holds them in his lap. "The shoot starts soon. Really soon. I have to be there for prep next week." He looks at me, trying to read how I feel about this. I'm happy for him, and I know he—we—need this. But I'm also aware of how Leo is long-distance. And what this means for our family.

"I guess we'll take a break from the clinic for the summer? We can't afford it now anyway." I feel a ruffle of irritation from Leo.

"I actually had an idea, not sure if you'll hate it," he says.

I shouldn't have brought up the clinic, but it's the first thing that comes to mind. "OK."

"I was thinking maybe you'd come out to the beach for the summer. You can work remote, and your parents will love it, you won't be alone, and you can come to New York for a few weeks."

He pauses, let's go of my hands. "The extra money might be really nice."

I know it bothers Leo that we don't have more. And it always hurts me when I see him up at night, hunched over his computer, like he can will the funds into our bank account from out of his fingers.

"What extra money?"

Leo gets sheepish. He closes one eye and looks at me. "I thought we could Airbnb out West Hollywood?"

I don't say anything, and he jumps in with more.

"We'd find great tenants, obviously. I figure I'll give it a deep clean, maybe patch up some paint spots. It's a good excuse to fix some things."

We've been talking about those renovations for two years, and we've never done a thing about them. It would be worth it to rent for that possibility alone.

"You've really been thinking about this."

Leo shrugs. "It's just an idea. It would help."

The thought of a stranger sleeping in our bed is instantly terrible, but then a moment later, fine.

"I like it," I say.

Leo's eyes brighten. "Really? Honestly we could probably make five grand."

"Two months? More than that."

He smiles at me. "My little optimist."

I bend my face up to kiss his lips. "I'll talk to my parents and Sylvia about it tomorrow. It would be nice to have some time with her."

Leo's hands find my low back. "You're amazing," he says. "Best wife ever." He starts to kiss me slowly, edging me back down against the sofa. "And I love you." He puts a hand against my rib cage, then moves it upward. "And I love your boobs."

They used to be a solid B cup, but since all the fertility treatments they hover at about a C+. I don't hate them, either.

Leo starts to tug at the hem of my shirt, trying to hike it up my torso. His fingers are impatient.

"Babe," I say. "We can't do it here."

Leo bends his face down to kiss the place where my neck and shoulder meet. "Oh, but we are."

I pull him toward me. I feel his hair—slightly greasy from the plane—and the stubble on his chin. I'm sure we have, I'm sure it hasn't been that long, but I'm struggling to remember the last time we had sex just because we wanted to. Not because I was ovulating or we were trying to top off an IUI or we were decimating from a failed retrieval. Sex has become, in a way, both an obligation and a rebellion.

Leo pauses.

"Are you OK?" he asks me. He can tell I've gone somewhere else.

I blink up at him. "I'm still waiting on the clinic," I say. "I mean, I know it didn't work."

I feel Leo immediately retract. "Jesus," he says.

"What?"

"Nothing."

"Just say it."

He sits up abruptly. I feel his hands leave my body.

"We said we wouldn't let this dictate our lives anymore."

"No, you said that," I say. I pull my arms around my chest.

"That's bullshit," he says. "You don't even believe it's worth it anymore. We know our odds, Laur. *You* just said it."

"Keep your voice down," I say, although he isn't yelling, not even a little bit.

"I'm so sick of pretending this is going to work out."

He sits back on the couch. He puts a hand over his mouth and exhales out through it. I feel my eyes sting up with tears.

"We can't control it," I say. "That's the point."

Next to me, he closes his eyes. "Yes, we can," he says. His head falls into his hands when he says what he does next. "We can just stop."

I feel my body grow cold. It's not the first time he's expressed this sentiment, not exactly, but it's the first time he's used those words this bluntly.

"I don't think it's fair that you're the only one who gets to choose," he says.

But I'm not choosing. That's what he doesn't understand. I have no choice. If I did, we wouldn't be here.

"Come on," he says. "Let's go to bed."

I don't want him to touch me. I don't even want to be near him. I feel betrayed. More than that, my body does. Because I'm the one who has to deal with the shots and the appointments and the saline tests that snake catheters up my cervix. Whose life is this dictating, exactly?

But I don't say anything. Instead, I let him lead me off the couch. I see our reflections in the glass window, two shadows backlit by the sea.

CHAPTER EIGHT

No one told her about the silver ticket until it was too late. She didn't know as a child, playing on the beach, watching the waves, wondering what would happen if she just walked out into the sea. She didn't know as a teenager, dealing with acne, and dating, and the perils of being a girl who grows up on the ocean but doesn't know a thing about the water—a man out of land, so to speak. She didn't know as a new bride, as a new mom—when she would have done anything to have someone tell her: *Don't worry, you can turn back the clock if you need to. Make a mistake, it won't hurt her, not really.*

No.

She finds out after the accident. After the death and destruction and the catatonic heartbreak—the love of her life, gone—her mother comes to her in the hospital. She tells her there is a way.

"You have a chance to take it back," Sylvia says. "You can undo it if you want to." She hands Marcella a small wooden box. Inside is a silver ticket.

"What is this?"

One of her mother's new age beliefs. More crystals, sage, bullshit. Marcella throws the box down on the floor.

"Pick it up," Sylvia says. And the way she says it—stern, focused, *capable*—makes Marcella wipe her eyes and do it.

She holds it in her hands.

Marcella has never had a particularly close relationship with Sylvia. After she was born she made Sylvia a single mother, which couldn't have been easy in the sixties, although she's never asked. They don't have that kind of relationship.

After they came to this country, Sylvia's mother met her father and they settled in Scarsdale, New York. He was a banker, and she never gave up the shoe business she'd inherited. They had some success together—not a lot, but you didn't need a lot in those days. It wasn't like it is now. You could get by on the middle.

Sylvia was raised in New York, and—as she tells it—the day she turned sixteen she loaded a car up with three suitcases and headed for the West Coast. She didn't have a particularly close relationship with her parents, but then again, Marcella never heard her say a bad word about them, either. Sylvia's mother was only twenty years her senior, but she was from a world so removed from the one her daughter was born into, there could have been a century between them.

Sylvia was beautiful—and beauty is currency. Marcella doesn't know a lot about the years in between leaving home and becoming a mother, but she does know that they brought success and adventure. Lots of it.

Marcella remembers her mother cooking at the beach, the hot oven open, Sylvia forgetting to turn it off but Marcella, somehow, knowing to stay away. She remembers the red kerchiefs Sylvia would tie on her head when they took out the convertible and the way they'd blow away in the wind. She remembers Donny and

Sam and Len Banks, who was her favorite. She remembers more than her mother believes she does.

Sylvia has always seemed so irresponsible to her, so out of touch. It was Marcella's job to follow behind, to make sure the doors were locked and the windows closed. She couldn't rely on Sylvia, not exactly, so she learned to rely on herself.

Standing in that hospital, though, Marcella understands that she needs to trust her mother. And she has no guidepost on how to do that. She has spent her adolescence making decisions in antithesis to what her mother believes, says, does. Trusting her now, believing her, is not an easy thing to do. It runs counterintuitive to the (successful) system Marcella has lived by forever.

But this was not in the plan. This grief, this early, surely is for someone else.

"You have had this ticket since the day you were born. It is your right to use if you want it. I had one, too."

Marcella looks at her bewildered, but something is already beginning to happen. She can feel the edges of this reality folding in, the softness of this hard-boiled hope.

"Think of the moment," Sylvia says. "Think of the moment you want to go back to."

Marcella closes her eyes. She thinks about a lot of things—the memories clamoring for top billing. She thinks about meeting Dave—the way he'd come up to her on the beach, right there, board in hand and asked if she wanted a beer. The way she took the bottle from out of his lips, the boldest thing she'd ever done.

The day that Lauren was born—quietly into the world at Cedars-Sinai hospital. The panic Marcella had had before she heard Lauren's first small, impish cry.

Big moments—wide, sweeping moments. Her wedding day. Dave's surf accident. The moment Lauren learned to walk, toddling in the kitchen, Marcella's arms extended wide. And then:

She thinks about the previous Sunday, at the house. How Dave had taken his board out early and how Lauren had stayed asleep. Marcella was rarely up before her, and when she went upstairs she peeked her head into her room and found her sleeping. She stood by the door like that for what felt like ten minutes. Lauren never let her be a mother anymore, never let her braid her hair or cuddle on the couch or put a cool hand to her forehead. Marcella misses it. Not that Lauren has ever let her do much—even as a child, she was always wriggling away, seeking independence, seeking the water, her father. But Marcella misses the closeness, still. The necessity by which mother and child are linked. The biological business of the whole thing.

Marcella didn't know whether Lauren was missing it, too, but she believed in that moment that she was and this hurt her—the fact that her child had a need she could no longer meet.

Dave came back then, barreling inside the house the way he always did—full steam, full volume. Wet from the water. Shaking like a dog absolutely everywhere.

She went down to warn him, *Be quiet, our child is asleep*, but when she got to him he swept her up into a loud, wet hug. She remembered feeling the salt of the sea on her cheek, the way she breathed in the familiar scent of him. And for whatever reason, in that moment, she didn't take it for granted. She knew how lucky she was to have this man hold her close to him.

"Honeydew, want to have breakfast? Is there coffee? The waves were off the hook this morning, wowwweee."

This is the moment she thinks about in that hospital. Inside her husband's arms, him asking about breakfast, her daughter safely asleep upstairs.

Isn't it always the mundane we want to return to when something catastrophic happens?

So she thinks about that memory, as Sylvia instructed her, she gets inside of it. And then, miraculously, she is back there.

There Dave is, dripping wet on the living room floor. There he is, asking for breakfast.

"Is there coffee? The waves were off the hook this morning, wowwweee."

Marcella screams. She keeps screaming. And hugging him. And kissing him.

Dave looks confused but only briefly. He screams back, still high off the ocean. He thinks it is just what they are doing: howling at the sun.

"With a welcome back like this, how am I supposed to not go out in the morning?"

And then Lauren comes down the steps. "What is going on?" she aasks. "Are you guys . . . OK?" She has on a white-striped T-shirt and yellow pajama pants. Her hair has come unspun from a ponytail—scattered straw.

Marcella throws her arms around her, stays that way. Lauren is still half asleep, maybe, and that's why she lets her. Marcella cannot remember the last time she held her daughter in her arms, and this closeness, this beating of her child's heart right here, right between her rib cage, makes Marcella weep.

"I love you," she says.

"God, Mom, enough. What is wrong with you?"

"I love my girls!" Dave bellows.

There is relief—puddles and pools of it. Relief that she has avoided tragedy. Relief that the past twelve hours are now just particles of memory, a memory that belongs only to her.

But the relief is not an ocean, cannot renew itself. It is like a saturated rainstorm, and eventually, when it dries up, in its place springs terror.

Marcella now knows that the unthinkable could happen, that it already has. And she also knows that next time she'd have no ability to stop it. No power, now, to save her husband.

Lauren still remembers that day, the one with the hug on the stairs. Although she does not know why it lingers so strongly in her memory.

CHAPTER NINE

I move into 31382 Broad Beach eleven days later, Pea in tow. It takes almost no time to find subletters—an actress who is out here shooting the pilot of a show on the Warner Bros. lot signed the day after we put it up on Airbnb. We're getting enough to cover our monthly payments and grab an extra fifty-five hundred dollars. Leo was right, it's a no-brainer.

The week after Leo leaves, a Wednesday, before I can even go to the clinic for blood work, I get my period. It's not a surprise, not exactly, but I feel this lost hope more than I do the others. Because I know I am running out of time. With my biological clock, yes, but also with Leo. We haven't talked about anything since that night at Broad Beach, and the weight of that—of this silence between us—feels like an elephant on my chest. I have no idea how we'll move forward.

I peel myself off the bathroom floor, and by Friday I'm hauling four suitcases and Pea's crate up the driveway and into Broad Beach.

Marcella greets me on the other side. "Honey," she says. "Are you sure about this?"

I feel a familiar jolt of irritation rocket through me. I point to the duffel in my hand. "It's a little late for that," I say. "Place is rented."

Sylvia appears in the doorway. She elbows Marcella. "Oh, what do you know, you've been cramping my style for sixty-nine years. Out of her way!"

I see Marcella take a step back, a flash of something cross her face. I hug Sylvia, as Marcella takes the crate out of my hand.

"Oh," Sylvia says. "You brought her."

"What was she supposed to do?" Marcella says. "Leave her?"

Sylvia has never much cared for animals, specifically cats. But there are no allergies to speak of in our family, and for the most part, Pea keeps to herself. My mother loves her—I think because Sylvia never let her have a pet of her own when she was younger.

"Upstairs," Sylvia says. "And watch the walls! I just had them repainted."

I take the steps up to my childhood bedroom. The walls are covered in family portraits. Black-and-whites of the older generations and full color as the years turn on. Sylvia and Mom on the beach; me holding a fish on a dock at the Jersey Shore, that summer we decided to trade one sand for another. Dad and I on our boards, our fingers in shakas. They are all in mismatched, wood-peeling frames. It's impossible to keep anything new with this much sunlight—eventually even the glass starts to bleach.

I pop the door at the top of the stairs open with my elbow. Inside it's like a time capsule. My things aren't there anymore—Sylvia loves clutter but not junk (her words), but everything else is exactly as it always was. There's my brass bed, Laura Ashley yellow floral sheets and curtains that once matched but are now so sun-soaked you can barely see the outline of a print. It smells musty and salty—exactly the scent of home.

Marcella follows me up, sets Pea's crate down and opens the door. The cat stretches and then disappears.

"We probably won't see her again all summer," I say.

"That'll thrill Grandma." Marcella sticks her hands on her hips and surveys the room. "Can I get you anything?"

"I'm good," I say. "I'm just going to unpack."

She leaves, and I drop my suitcases and flop myself down on the bed. The springs creak—unused to weight.

I take out my phone and hit Leo's number. It's the third time I've called today, and I'm not expecting him to answer, so it's a nice surprise when he does. He was kind and gentle when I got my period, but I feel the distance between us—all the things we can't take back.

"Hey," Leo says. "You make it out?"

"Just got here."

I walk to the window and peel the curtain back. The sun is shining high overhead—it's noon at the beach. I can feel the outside calling, practically mocking me to get out of the stuffy house.

Through the phone I hear the sounds of Manhattan traffic. "How's your day been?" I ask.

"Just coming up for air. We've been location scouting since seven. Did you know there's a private library uptown where the books have grown into the walls? It's all outside; they're covered in ivy. It's apparently one of the wonders of Manhattan."

He seems engaged, excited. I'm glad. That's what he should feel if we're spending this summer apart. That the job is worth it.

"No idea," I say. "I didn't even know there were wonders of Manhattan."

"Apparently. It was incredible. We should do that in our house."

Leo is always talking about this fictional home we will have someday. This three-million-dollar house in West Hollywood with a full backyard and a fireplace and now an outdoor library.

I hear a car honk loudly, and the sound of a siren going by. "Hang on," he says. "Just waiting for them to pass."

After another moment, the noise dies down.

"This place is a maniac," Leo says.

I imagine him, jeans and a T-shirt, a week's worth of stubble and sweat stains, lumbering through the streets of Manhattan. Leo belongs in the Pacific Northwest with a beer and sixty-two-degree temps.

"What are you going to do tonight?" I ask.

"A few of the crew are posting up at a bar in Midtown. Thought I'd join them for a pint."

Leo's British sneaks in sideways. He uses *knackered* and the trash can is always the *bin*.

"That sounds fun," I say. "Call me after."

"Will do. Love ya."

He hangs up before I can reciprocate.

I toss the duffel and suitcases into the closet without opening them, pull on a blue Nike one-piece bathing suit from where it lives in a drawer, and pad downstairs.

My mother is in the kitchen chopping lettuce leaves from the garden. The most cooking she does is the kind that doesn't involve a stovetop or oven. She assembles. "Going for a swim?" she asks me. She doesn't look up.

"We'll see. I might just take a walk."

I think about inviting her, but she looks busy.

"Do you want a wet suit? Your father has a million. The water is freezing right now."

"This is hardly freezing." I pop a cherry tomato into my mouth from a bowl that sits on the counter. "I have a spring suit around here somewhere. I'll find it."

She blinks and looks at me, shakes her head. "Whatever you want."

My relationship with my mom has always been like a dance I haven't quite memorized. We move around each other, sometimes together, often stumbling away or stepping on each other's toes. I used to look at people who were best friends with their mothers and wonder what that would be like—to feel so universally and wholly understood by another person. I know she loves me, but love is given, easy. I have never been certain she likes me—that she doesn't judge every decision I make through a lens of *why*.

"I'll see you later," I say, and slip out the back door. I see her watching me through the glass with curiosity and something else, too. Something that feels . . . heated. I turn my back on her before I can place it, and take the stairs down.

CHAPTER TEN

The beach is hot, and, yes, the water is cold. The Pacific Ocean should be warm—it's the water of sunny California—but the circulation patterns mean the sea filters from Alaska, and it's always a little bit biting.

I dip my toe in and am pierced by that immediate, icy thrill. In California, we surf all year long. I remember forty-degree days when we'd be out on the water. You just grin and bear it. It only hurts on the way in, not the way out, and eventually, you just get used to it.

Wading in is torturous, even in the summer, and as soon as the tide exhales I push past the break and dive under the waves. It feels delicious—like swimming in the deep, deep sea even though I'm nearly at the water's edge.

I come to the surface and shake out my hair and see my dad taking the steps, following my trail. I watch him lumber down, pausing once to rub his knee. He sits on the bottom step and sips from a blue ceramic water bottle. He has a T-shirt on I recognize—three pineapples, all in sunglasses. When he sees me seeing him, he waves. I wave back.

"You coming in?" I call.

He shakes his head. "Just watching ya!"

I do a few laps, back and forth, letting my body glide through the water, feeling the thump and hum of my blood as my heart rate accelerates. There's a sweet spot once you're in where your body adjusts to the temperature and it feels like gliding through velvet. Stay in too long, and you start to pickle.

When you're surfing, it's all action. You're running a marathon out on the water. Even without a wet suit, I never think about the temperature when I'm in motion. But just my own body in the waves is a different thing. The clock runs out fast.

I get out of the water and wring my hair into the sand. Dad waves again, and I walk up and take a seat next to him, wrapping myself in the towel he hands me.

"Sorry," I say, as water drips all over his blue T-shirt and board shorts. He responds by slinging his arm around me and pulling me into a wet shoulder hug.

"I'll live."

We watch the beach. The waves are usually choppy midday—shitty surf condition—but today the ocean is almost pancaked.

"It's nice to have you back," Dad says, releasing me.

"It's nice to be back."

"Silver lining to your husband being away—your old man gets a revival."

~~~

When I first introduced my parents to Leo it was at Taverna Tony—Malibu's resident Greek restaurant in the Cross Creek shopping center. My parents almost never eat out. For one, all the restaurants in Malibu are overpriced, and for the other, my dad says the best spot in town is the one they've got. *The food is spectacular, and you can't beat the view.*

Marcella can arrange a salad, and Dave knows his way around the barbecue, but they get their restaurant-quality meals because of Sylvia. I don't blame them for wanting to stay put.

But my parents knew Leo was special and insisted their first meeting should be somewhere special, too.

Taverna Tony is a huge restaurant complete with a bougainvillea-twined terrace and belly dancers after dark.

"It's an experience," my dad likes to say. He loves it there. The waiters all know him by name, and he gets the dip for free—which in and of itself, for him, is a reason to go.

That first night, Leo and I were early, and we were shown to a table on the patio. It was a cool summer night—Malibu never gets that hot in the evening, not even in the dead of July. I had on a silver slip dress and a denim jacket. Leo was wearing khakis and a short-sleeved button-down. I remember thinking he looked handsome—better than I'd ever seen him—and then chiding myself that I liked when he was dressed out of the norm for him. When he was buttoned up, playing at someone else—a collar, a pant with structure.

"They're going to love you," I told him. I gave his hand a firm squeeze.

"I hope so."

"Why wouldn't they? Everyone loves you."

Leo shrugged. "Most people like me. But your parents are serious."

"Who said that?"

Leo looks at me. "I can just tell. You wouldn't be this nervous otherwise." Leo took my face in his hands. He kissed me.

My parents came then, so I didn't have time to tell him he was wrong. They weren't serious. At least, my dad wasn't. It's just that so few people had folded into my family before. That it has been me and them for such a long time. That I was worried about including him this late in the game—when so much had already happened, so much he'd never be able to experience because it was context now.

"Honey!" My dad threw his arms around me. My parents had come without Sylvia, who had her standing card game. Her card game is serious: If you miss two in a row, you're out for good, and the month before she'd been down with a cold.

"She apologizes," my mother said, and I wondered if it was strange to Leo to note a grandparent's absence from a meet-the-parents dinner.

Marcella took in Leo. "It's really nice to meet you," she said.

Leo ran a hand through his hair. "Yeah, same. You, too."

Dad ordered a beer, Mom a glass of Sancerre.

"Lauren tells me you're a photographer," my mother said. She sipped her wine, two interlocking shawls cascading over her shoulders. That night she had on a mauve linen dress under the outerwear. She looked softer somehow.

"Sort of," Leo said. "I mean, yes. But I'm a DP."

My mom looked at my dad. Neither of them had any idea what he meant, and I felt momentarily annoyed that Leo had used the acronym. *Just tell them. This isn't their world.*

"Director of photography," I said.

"Right," Leo jumped in. "I help a director shoot the film, or television show—whatever it may be. I'm responsible for a shot list—really the whole creative direction of the piece."

Leo was prideful about his art, sometimes it came off as slightly arrogant. I didn't care—hadn't cared—because I assumed this was how all photographers felt. This was how all artists felt. But sitting there with my parents I felt like I suspected they did—that he was being purposefully obtuse. Leaving us out of an experience we clearly couldn't relate to.

"How exciting," my mother said.

"It will be," Leo said, and I felt his affability creeping back in. "I'm working on building my career, truth be told. I was an assistant director for a long time. And only moved into photography recently. It's really where I belong, but I have to pay my dues."

I felt instant relief at his vulnerability. My mother smiled.

"I don't know if Lauren has told you but I was a teacher," she said.

Leo leaned his elbows on the table, grateful, I thought, to have the spotlight off him for a moment. "No, she didn't mention it."

My mom nodded. "Webster Elementary. I started when Lauren was about sixteen."

"Did you enjoy it?"

Dave laughed. "What a question!"

Marcella smiled. "Loved it. Taught second grade. It's a really interesting time. Children are becoming so aware of their environment and each other. There's a lot happening, and so much of it gets formed in the classroom."

Leo picked up his beer and took a sip. I could tell he was trying to follow her but wasn't sure where she was going with this, how it related to what came before.

"I always felt like it was where I belonged, in that classroom," she said. "I got a late start, but once I got there it was like everything clicked. It saved me, in a way." She took a small sip of water. "So I think it's wonderful when people pursue their passions."

Leo smiled. Ah. "Thank you, Marcella. I appreciate your sharing that."

One thing about Leo is he means what he says. I felt his genuine warmth pervade the table. I put my hand on his knee and squeezed.

"Why did you end up retiring?" he asked.

Marcella shook her head. "I don't know—it just got harder. I probably shouldn't have, if you want to know the truth, but it's tough these days. Parents want their kids to be guaranteed Harvard admission at eight."

I remember thinking it was funny she'd critique that because that was how she felt, too, wasn't it? She wanted me to go to a good college, wanted me to succeed at something. Academics was important to her—more important than it was to my dad.

"It's nuts," Leo said. "You'd think with rising depression rates they'd just want them to be happy."

Marcella nodded slowly. "I didn't feel like I could connect with students in the way I was used to. I found myself watching too many of my words. Maybe I stopped trying as hard."

I remember the years when my mom taught. In many ways teaching was the thing that helped her reconnect to the world, that gave her a path forward after the accident. She'd come home with stories about her classroom—the kids loved her, and rather than feeling jealous I felt proud. I loved that other students saw her, saw the parts of her that made a great instructor—that made her a great mom. Because she was that. No one knew how to impart the rules quite like my mother.

She taught up until I was out of college, at least. Although in that moment at dinner, I remember thinking I didn't remember when she stopped.

A waiter came by and delivered sheep's milk cheese with triangles of warm, doughy pita, and Taverna Tony's signature spread—half hummus, half cream cheese and olives. Dave beamed proudly.

"Thanks, Ivan."

We dug in. Leo is not a shy eater—he loves food. On one of our first dates he took me on a taco crawl of the east side of LA. I have a strong stomach, always have, and I liked the way Leo respected my appetite. I didn't feel like I had to be shy taking down tacos or pulling apart ribs with him. The more I ate, the more he loved it.

I looked at Marcella. I could tell she wasn't finished with what she had to say. And I felt a pang of sympathy for her—that we were all prioritizing our hunger over what she was trying to share. I was surprised at how I wanted to get back to it, too. I wanted her to be able to sell herself in this capable and gentle light.

"Parents can be total assholes," Leo said, through a mouthful of pita, somewhat unprompted.

Marcella hates swearing—but then I looked at her face. She had a small, slightly pulled smile on. She was trying not to laugh.

"They really can," she said.

Leo reached across the table and offered his fist, and Marcella, impossibly, bumped it.

I looked at my dad, who was laughing into his beer.

That was it, they loved him.

Dinner was charcoal-grilled octopus, roasted eggplant puree, tangy grape leaves, lamb souvlaki, and Greek salad.

"My favorite is the moussaka," my mom said, serving herself more of the layered eggplant, beef, and béchamel. "I never eat anything this rich, except here."

I made a face. Moussaka is decidedly not my favorite. Leo clocked it.

"More for me and your mom," he said, taking the serving spoon from Marcella's hand. She and Leo exchanged a glance. She wasn't looking at me, she wasn't even talking to me, but I felt more connected to her than I had in years. In that moment, we were just any other mother and daughter, meeting the new boyfriend.

My father ate the octopus, eggplant, and salad. He steered clear of the lamb. He's always been cognizant of his cholesterol—he had open-heart surgery thirty years ago to fix two clogged arteries. He had been only thirty-nine, practically unheard of. Dad's diet changed radically after. He was mostly vegan for a while, then added in some lean meats. My mother joined him at first, but then slid back into her favorites as the years went on—although in solidarity there is still no "real" milk in their fridge. I know it's been a learning curve for her to cook for him—Sylvia, too. They are used to heavy oils, and a pad of butter for the pot.

"Well, that was excellent," Leo said when we finished.

He fought my dad on the bill, which I'd asked him to, but it still made me happy anyway. Dave refused.

"Next time we'll try the spare ribs," Marcella said.

Leo smiled at her. "You're on."

After dinner we said good night to them and drove home along the silver water. The sun had long since set, and the road was wide open—just a few taillights a long way in the distance. The radio was on. I heard Van Morrison hum softly through the speakers.

"They're really nice," Leo said, taking my hand. We were in his old Subaru, affectionately named Berta. "Your mom is funny."

I thought back to whether anyone had ever described Marcella that way. She had loved Stone, but in the way you love the boy you've watched grow up—she was invested in *him*, I thought. Not necessarily our relationship.

Had I ever seen her smile that much? Banter with someone? Eat two platefuls of cream sauce?

"I've never seen her like that," I said to Leo. "She loved you. It's important to both of them that they get along with who I'm with. We're close."

It was both true and it wasn't. We were the kind of family whose narrative could only be that of closeness, but were we actually close? My mother didn't know the contents of my wardrobe. I didn't call her when I had a rash or a fever to ask her what to do. If the roof leaked, they never found out. I'd spent my teenage years arching away from her, and years after observing her from a distance while we both worried about my dad.

Maybe having a partner was a way to get closer, to come to them as an equal, two for two. There would be someone else to open the door.

In the car that night, driving back along the ocean, I felt something well up in me that I wouldn't quite name. I wanted him to like them, yes, but more importantly, I wanted him to love them. I wanted him to call my dad up for work advice and share recipes and restaurant recommendations with my mom. I wanted his natural ease—the part of him that drew me to him like a magnet—to penetrate us. I wanted him to transform us, to make us that easeful, too.

I wanted to share my parents—the weight of them—with someone else. But I wanted them to be less heavy in the transformation. I wanted Leo to fix it, whatever this thing was between Marcella and me that had come out broken. And I wanted him to make it OK when the unthinkable happened, someday. When I would be here alone.

"It was just our first dinner, right?" Leo said. He had no attitude, no resentment or impatience. He was just stating a fact. The stakes weren't that high. It was one dinner. "I'm hopeful there will be a lot more." He took my hand. I felt something relax in me that had been stiff for a long time.

"We'll go out there next weekend," I said. "You can see the house."

Leo kissed the back of my palm. From above us the wind blew my hair everywhere.

"Whatever you want," he said, and I knew that he meant it.

CHAPTER ELEVEN

The next morning I give up on sleep around five. The upside to this is that I'm able to exchange some texts with Leo, who is already up and location scouting in Brooklyn. Once he stops responding—must have found somewhere good—I hook my bathrobe around me and plod downstairs.

Dad is at the coffee machine, board shorts and an old Quicksilver sweatshirt on, worn at the collar.

"You going out?" I ask. The last word turns into a yawn, and I reach into the cabinet behind him and pull down a mug.

"Nah," he says. "Gonna do some morning pages."

Dad is a family lawyer, yes, but he's also a writer. Twelve mystery books under the pen name Irene Stills. He's been publishing since I was in middle school. A neighbor at the beach was a big literary agent at WME, and one day out on the water, Dad asked if he could give her something. They sold the first novel six weeks later.

Dad's books sell modestly. He has a small cult following that comes out to every local tour he does—mostly Pages in Manhattan Beach and Vroman's in Pasadena. Simon & Schuster always buys his next book. He loves it, and it's nice extra money. Not enough to renovate a beach house, but enough to take a vacation once a year, handle some repairs, and buy Mom a nice piece of jewelry.

"My Monopoly money," he calls it.

Dad hands me the pot, and I pour. It's extra dark this morning. Dad has never been a great coffee maker—he's inconsistent. No matter how many times we tell him—*four scoops and an extra for the pot*—it never comes out even.

"But you should," he says.

"What?" I ask, although I know. His response catches me off guard.

Dad raises his eyebrows at me. "When was the last time you paddled out?" He takes a sip of his coffee. "Your board is still here, you know."

I feel a familiar clench in my stomach. Surfing was always a point of contention for my mom with my father. Too dangerous, too much risk—*too much downside*. Over time I came to understand what she meant. If something happened out there, would his heart be strong enough to get him to safety? People who have multiple bypasses before forty shouldn't push their cardiovascular limits.

But after the accident, Dad doubled down. He wanted to be out on the water even more—and he wanted me with him. "We can't live in fear," he'd tell my mom, and she'd just shake her head.

"We can't live like fools, either."

By that time what either of them thought didn't matter. I was already hooked, and surfing was no longer just the story of me and my dad but the story of me and Stone.

Every inch of this shoreline, every molecule of water, reminds me of us. The way the tide recedes in the summer and leaves a huge swath of shoreline for walking, the break of the waves at

Lechuza Cove in the winter, the way the spray hits the rocks at sunset. When we broke up I tried to keep going out—surfing wasn't just Stone's thing; it was also mine, who I was—but I couldn't bring myself to do it. The water suddenly transformed. What I once understood, felt, lived, now felt foreign in a way I couldn't quite grasp. And ignorance on the water is dangerous.

I gave it up completely about a year after we broke up.

But now—

Something about being here, coming down the stairs from my old bedroom, finding Dad in the kitchen, board on the deck, makes me feel almost as if I am retracing my childhood rhythms. Wake up, roll out, surf, school. I can feel myself being pulled backward, all the life that has occurred between then and now being unspooled.

I take another sip of hot coffee. It's as thick as mud this morning. I head to the refrigerator to pour some milk.

"It's pitch-black out," I say. "Don't know if that's the time for me to wade back in."

My dad waves his hand at me. "C'mon," he says. "You used to rule dawn patrol."

I shake the almond milk and pour. Dad comes over and slings an arm around my shoulder. He holds me to him, putting his head against my cheek.

"You know the water," he says. "You always have. You just forgot for a while. You gotta trust her again."

He releases me and picks up his laptop. "Your board is downstairs. Have fun."

I put my coffee in the sink—pouring out Dad's sludgy remains and remaking the pot with the appropriate measurements. I flick the machine on, so it'll be done when we're ready for refills—

and when Mom emerges a few hours from now. Then I go and change.

Pulling on my summer suit—basically just a bathing suit with long sleeves—feels like trying to wear a shower cap as a dress. It's been so long since I've tried to pour myself into this piece of latex. I'm sweating by the time it's on, beads running down my back and forehead. I give the zipper a final tug and head downstairs.

Below the kitchen is a room that essentially functions as a storage unit. All the furniture, art, appliances, and hobbies that we've discarded over the years line the walls. I spot my board, stacked behind some paintings of Sylvia's. It looks cleaner than it should, considering it's been more than a decade since I've taken it out.

I grab some wax off the table, hook the board under my arm, and walk down the steps. It's chilly outside, and the board is heavy—I don't lift much these days, and whatever exercise I do is brief and light. I feel its weight underneath me, the weight of this adventure, and I almost bail, put it back, pour myself another cup, and grab my phone—but instead I push on.

When I get to the sand I set the long board down, put on some fresh wax. As I draw crisscrosses on the board I start to feel my arms relax. I know how to do this. I rub rail to rail two times over, careful not to apply too much pressure, and then I toss what's left of the wax down and strap on my leash.

Dad was right—there are perfect offshore winds and head-high waves. Ideal conditions. In the winter, Broad Beach can bring in some killer waves—but they're big. The summer is a great time to get back out there with some nice two-to-three-foot waves.

I try to think about the last time I was on my board, but the memory is hazy—I had no idea the last time I went out would be the last time, so it was unremarkable.

Come on, Lauren. In.

I push the board into the water and hop on. And as soon as I'm belly down, I start to paddle.

I can feel the ocean around me—icy and yet inviting. This is not a foreign place; this is *my* place. For the first twenty-five years of my life my home was in this water.

My body starts to remember. My breath syncs up with my arms, and before long I'm in that mediative trance. I remember the early years, the "paddle, don't scream" years, when an oncoming wave would send a little thrill of terror down my middle, and I find myself repeating the mantra again and again as I move through the water. *Paddle, don't scream; paddle, don't scream; paddle, don't scream.* One two push, one two push, one two push.

It takes about three minutes to get to the lineup. The lineup is where the main break and takeoff spot is, and it's called that because it's where the surfers literally line up. We hang on our boards, waiting for the next set. Sometimes you hang back, behind the peak, if the lineup is deep. Or on the ends, and ride the scraps.

I'm winded by the time I get out there, practically panting. I sit up and straddle my board, letting my feet dangle into the water.

There are five other surfers out today—not a lot, considering the conditions. But Broad Beach—while not secret—is a lesser populated surf spot. Other beaches in Malibu can be crowded. At Zuma during a swell the lineup will be twenty deep. And then you're fighting for waves. That's why I've always loved it here. Not the best waves, no. But hidden enough.

There's a local hierarchy to the lineup in Malibu—like in most places. If you're a newbie, you gotta wait your turn. The regulars get the first waves even if they've been chilling the shortest amount of time. Dad's a regular. No one would dare drop in on one of Dave's waves. But right now, I'm a tourist here. There was a time I knew every single person with a board on the whole coast of Malibu. Not anymore. I move to the left of the peak, more toward the tail, giving the other surfers space, expressing my respect.

I bob up and down, stretch my arms a little.

"Oy!"

Something instinctive hits my sternum and then—there Stone is, paddling out to me. He waves to two kids who I've never seen before, guys who can't be a day older than eighteen.

"Laur!" he says. "No shit. You're here."

I haven't heard him call me a nickname in so long. The familiarity is foreign.

Stone gestures for me to come in a little closer. I glance at the guys but they just nod. I swivel my board around and paddle to them.

"Hi, yeah."

Stone nods with approval. "How long's it been?"

"A while." I give the boys a small wave. "I'm Lauren."

"Right on," one of them says. "Bert. This is Kai."

Neither of them are wearing any kind of rash guard—just board shorts. A lot of the younger surfers refuse the coverage—they think they're superhuman.

"You guys probably know her pops," Stone says. "Dave Novak?"

One of them reaches over and pushes the other one in the side. "We love Dave! Dude can rip."

I feel my chest swell. The image of my father—strong and vibrant—fills me with a certain kind of pride and security. Dad can still rip.

"Is this the right spot?" Kai asks. He looks down the shore, uncertain.

"Nah, man, we not doing that again. Every time we paddle to another peak we miss it."

Bert and Kai start to squabble, and Stone turns his attention to me.

"It's nice to see you out here," he says. "You come on the weekends these days?"

I shake my head. It's wild to me that he doesn't know I don't surf anymore, that I haven't been out since it was us together. That to me the water is ours when it so clearly isn't for him.

And then I hear Bert shout. "Oui!"

A wave is incoming. Stone and Kai paddle into it.

"Ho!" Stone says, warning Kai not to drop in on him.

I duck-dive under the wave and come up to see Stone riding it in.

"Dude!" Bert says. He looks at me sympathetically. *Better luck next time.*

I spit out some salt water and keep my eye on the horizon.

The second wave of the set comes in. I start to paddle against it, hard as I can.

"All yours," Kai says. "Let's go, surfer girl!"

My arms move, I'm hardly looking, and then I feel that familiar hovering, and I put my hands on either side of the board and pop up into a crouch. I drop to the bottom after takeoff and then come up and hit the lip as I move down the line. I'm inside a wave for the first time in ten years, but I can't even think about that—I can't think about anything but my stance and core and the movement of the board.

I'm right here. And there is nothing but space. Even time doesn't have a place here. It's total and complete presence. *That's* why we love it. No past, no future. There isn't even awareness. The second you think about anything but your breath, it's over. But man, those few seconds. There's nothing like it.

I fall into the water at the tail end, grateful for the refresh, and come up to see Stone paddling fast toward me.

"Shit," Stone calls. "You been surfing in your dreams or something?" He reaches me, a little out of breath. "How long have you really been out of commission?"

I'm winded and shocked. I feel simultaneously wrung out and high on adrenaline. It was a tiny wave—not tunnel, but still. I forgot this hit. I forgot how good it is. There are no problems out here—no financial strain, no infertility, no husband across the country ignoring my text messages.

"I don't know," I say.

"Well, you killed that," he says. "How did it feel?"

I shake my head, my breath still coming in fits and spurts. I pull myself up onto my board and straddle it. We're getting tossed around by the break, but I don't care. It feels great. No, it feels better than that. It feels like elation.

"Epic," I say.

Stone reaches over and holds my board steady. I feel us begin to float together—*whoosh whoosh whoosh*. It sends me straight back to our last morning here.

We paddled out like we always did, first thing, before the sunrise. We were twenty-five then. We'd been surfing the same break for almost a decade, but since I'd gone to USC for college we'd been out less and less. I was out of practice; I wasn't as in step with him as I used to be.

We'd been in bed that morning at Bonnie and Jeff's house when he told me. Stone had the whole downstairs, and their place was and is spectacular. A thirty-million-dollar McMansion—a floor for everyone.

"I'm moving to Boulder," he said. "I decided I'm going to do it."

I remember not knowing what he meant. *Move. Boulder. What?*

We were naked. His chest was bare, and so was mine. He rolled onto his side and rubbed the curve of my back.

"I have to get out of here," he said. "I want to start Board Up, and I think I've figured out how there."

I just looked at him. I still couldn't quite compute. "Here is me," I said.

He exhaled. "Laur, it's not. Here is the fact that I'm doing absolutely nothing with my life."

"You're twenty-five," I said to counter. I knew Stone was restless. I knew that when he dropped out of SMU he moved back in with no plan and things had more or less remained that way. My mom often said that Stone's fatal flaw was that he'd never have to work a day in his life. I thought she was ridiculous. Who cared about work? He could surf, and he would. It had felt like enough. It had been enough. It was all he ever wanted—me and the ocean.

"I don't want to be a beach bum for the rest of my life," he said.

I felt breathless with the sting. The rejection of everything that made up our life together.

"So don't. Go back to school, get a job in town. There are a million things you could do here. Why do you have to move to Boulder to do something?"

As if Boulder was the only place to have a real life. Stone didn't even like the cold! He complained when it was sixty-five degrees outside. I remember thinking then that this was just a passing idea—like when people take up gardening, buy new gloves and pots, and then abandon the whole thing a month later. He'd get over it, move on. The plane ticket would never materialize.

"Come with me," he said.

I had just started as an assistant at Shatz and Steinberg, the CPAs who worked for half of Hollywood. I hated it.

"We'll get a little house. I'll start Board Up." He looked at me. I could tell he was genuine because Stone was a terrible liar. "We could have a baby."

I blinked at him.

We could have a baby just hung there.

It was appealing in the way grown-up life is appealing when you're very young. When everything feels like pretend, like the best version of itself. When a house and a baby is cardboard and plastic and you think it's romantic to get by on very little. When love is enough, really, because it's all in theory anyway.

I wanted to go with him because I was in love with him. He had been my constant for so long—as long as I could remember, really. I had no idea how I'd do life without him. But I also knew, somehow, that I would. That I was not going to be the kind of girl who marries her first love. That even though our relationship was so very real—ten years!—it wasn't permanent. It's just that every time I thought about this particular inevitability, it was so far in the future it could have been someone else.

"I can't," I said. "My parents—"

It had been ten years since my dad's accident, and while I didn't remember it—none of us did but my mom—I knew that life that far outside of this place was not for me. I didn't feel like I could leave them, if it came right down to it. Whether that was for them or for me, I didn't know. I wanted a life separate from them, but I wanted them in sight.

Stone said nothing. It occurred to me that he could be reconsidering. That maybe now was the moment's he'd say everything I knew he felt: "Never mind, dumb idea. What do you want for breakfast?"

But instead he was silent.

"Stone," I said. "Are you for real?"

I saw his eyes fill up. And I wanted to roll closer to him, bury my face in his chest, and smell that smell that was so uniquely him—sex, wax, and salt water and something else liquid, like gasoline. Something that could burn up the whole room.

He turned on his back and looked up at the ceiling. When he finally spoke, it was barely a whisper.

"I need to go," he said. "I have to do this. I've already found the space."

I wasn't angry. Maybe I should have been, but there were parts of Stone I knew I didn't have access to. There were parts of him maybe I didn't want access to. When you're that in love you don't want to sacrifice a piece of it to reality. We were used to seeing each other so intimately up close that it was easy to ignore how all the details hung together.

"Let's get wet," he said.

"Stone," I said, "We should talk about this." I didn't want to, I just knew it was what grown-ups did, and I wanted us to be grown-ups now. We weren't sixteen anymore.

"Then let's do it in the water."

In six minutes we were paddling out. We broke up out on the water. We did everything out on the water.

Now I look at Stone holding my board—and I feel something

rise up in me. I'm out of breath from the run and aware of my body—all the pieces that used to work together that don't anymore but that maybe still could, with enough time.

"You miss it," Stone says. He's smiling slightly. The edges of his mouth curl upward.

It's not a question, but I answer anyway.

"Yeah," I say. "I guess I do."

CHAPTER TWELVE

When we climb out of the water my legs feel like Jell-O. And I'm thirsty. And starving. Stone carries his board up and then comes back for mine. I let him carry it up our stairs and deposit it on the deck.

We've been out for hours—at least two. The sun is high overhead now, the temperature already creeping up into the eighties.

I turn on the outdoor shower.

"OK if I stash this here for the time being?" Stone points to his board, right next to mine.

"No problem."

"You mind if I dip?" he asks, gesturing to the shower.

"Go for it."

He pulls his rash guard off, revealing the toned and tanned chest I saw the other day. And then he dips his head into the stream and shakes out his hair.

I watch him under the water. He leans his face in, sucks in some water, and then spits it out. He moves his body in a semicircle under the stream, picks up both feet, and then cocks his head at me.

"Damn," he says. "That'll do it. Go for it."

He steps aside, and I get under the faucet. It's freezing, but it feels great. My body is used to the cold now.

I pull my suit down—I always wear a bikini top underneath—and get some water on my skin. Stone hands me a towel as I turn off the spigot.

We towel off in silence for a few minutes until my stomach rumbles. Loud enough for us both to hear.

"Want to get breakfast?" Stone asks.

"Take me to food," I say.

Half an hour later we're seated at Paradise Cove Beach Cafe. The place gets touristy later in the day, but in the mornings it's all locals. A white, wide-windowed building that's half indoors and half outdoors, Paradise Cove is parked right on the ocean. There's also a beach club where visitors can rent chairs for the day, though we've never done that.

We choose a table in the sand under a white umbrella. I'm wearing shorts and a sweatshirt, the back half of which is damp from my still-wet hair. Stone has on a blue T-shirt and some khaki linen pants. He ran home to change, then came and picked me up five minutes later.

The Paradise Cove Beach Cafe has been here for as long as I can remember. It's run by a family that used to own the entire cove of the beach, back in the fifties and sixties, when Malibu was nothing more than a casual, kickback community. I love this place. I've been coming here since childhood, and it hasn't changed much, which is more than can be said for most of the coast. Like most beach enclaves, there's some tension between the haves and the have-nots—or the ones who've held out and the ones who have taken the place of those who didn't. People see Malibu as a billionaire's playground, and it is, to a certain extent—so many old-timers have closed up shop and moved on, rents too high, buyouts too juicy. But it's also still, and always will be, home to a long and casual history of spots just like this one. That's the Malibu I know and love. The "no shirt, no shoes, no problem" Malibu.

I slurp up a second water and a coffee. He sips from an iced vanilla latte. The remains of our breakfast are splayed out before us—toast and eggs Benedict and pancakes and every side on the menu. That's what it's like after surfing—no talking, just eating. I snap off the last remaining piece of bacon and then wipe down my fingers on a paper napkin, satisfied.

I get no reception down here, and I'm aware of my phone in my bag. I haven't spoken to Leo yet today. I called him while I changed, but he didn't answer. Leo is a black-iced-coffee guy, even in winter, and it gives me some small pleasure to see Stone's glass of complicated sugar.

"I forgot how many pancakes you can take down," Stone says.

"Me, too," I say.

Stone loops an arm over the back of the chair next to him and teeters it onto two legs. He looks right across the table at me.

"Can't believe you stayed away for so long."

I hold his gaze for a beat. "How's Bonnie today?"

Stone releases the chair. "I don't know. She was sleeping when I left, but I feel like we're getting closer." He closes his eyes briefly.

I reach across the table and pat his forearm. "I'm so sorry."

It feels nice to be there for him. Easy. I think about all the times I've done it before.

He gives me a little smile.

"Yeah," he says. "It's a terrible disease."

I don't know what else to say. I pick up my water. "How is your dad dealing?"

Stone shakes his head. "Total denial. He doesn't want to acknowledge what's happening. He booked a trip for them to Baja in September. I can't say I blame him."

I run a pinky down the edge of my water glass. The beads of condensation bleed onto the table. "It must be impossible."

Stone nods. "Life, right? It is impossible. For so many people."

Now is not the first time I've thought about my responsibility. Whether I owe the world this ticket, and whether it makes me a bad person to not save someone else's life.

I could fix it, couldn't I? If I went back far enough. Maybe she would still get cancer but they'd have the time again. I could convince Stone to get her a better scan, enter more clinical trials earlier. I could tell them what would happen—they could cut it off at the pass. She'd have a chance.

"Hey," Stone says. He reaches across the table and play-slaps his hand against my shoulder. "You good?"

"Yeah," I say. "I'm just very sorry. I know how much you love Bonnie. I love her, too. I haven't seen her in a long time, but I always loved being around her."

When we were kids—way before we ever got together—Bonnie was the mom whose house you wanted to visit. She didn't bake, couldn't be bothered, but she always had a pantry stocked with snacks. The real stuff—Oreos and Chips Ahoy and rows of peppermint patties. Our house had one cookie jar filled with oatmeal raisin and granola bars that Sylvia baked. Stone's house was Candy Land.

Whenever I saw Bonnie she'd always ask me what I was reading. Bonnie loved books, and she'd read almost anything. Whatever she found at Diesel in Brentwood or Pages in Manhattan Beach or Target or even Costco. She read every #1 *New York Times* bestseller, even the ones by Patterson.

"Is she still reading?" I ask, and feel something pinch right behind my sternum. I don't want the answer, I realize.

"A little," he says. "It's easier when I read to her. We've been going back through Harry Potter together."

"She loved those."

Stone holds his gaze to mine. "She loved you."

We were so young when we were together that we threw the word around like a kind of hot potato. Neither of us wanted to hold on to it for too long.

"I'd love to see her," I say. "If you think she'd want a visitor."

Stone nods. "You're always welcome, Lauren. You know that."

Our check comes, Stone pays, and then we're climbing back into his Bronco. Hawaiian reggae blares through the speakers. We drive up the canyon, back to the highway. I run my hand out the window, feeling the weight of the wind, like water.

CHAPTER THIRTEEN

Stone pulls into his parents' driveway. I look through the glass panes on either side of the door. I can see just a fragment of their living room—recently redecorated. It bears no resemblance to the interior I once knew, but why would it? I haven't been inside in ten years.

We get out of the car, and Stone notices me hovering.

"Do you want to come in?" he asks.

"Do you want to check first?" I can feel my heartbeat quicken. There's a part of me that doesn't want to see her. To see her like this.

"It'll make her day," he says. "Come on."

Stone pulls the door open—a big oak with a brass handle—and then we are inside.

The house opens into an entryway. There is a coatrack that hangs with sweaters and a raincoat, and a line of shoes by the door—mostly what I assume are Stone's, and two pairs of slippers. Past the entry is the living room. When we were young it was all Ralph Lauren florals, but now it's cool blues and whites—a classic beach house, serene and well-appointed.

I drop my voice to a whisper. "The house looks great."

Stone smiles. "Bonnie redecorated a couple of years ago. I like it, too."

"Honey?" a quiet voice calls. "Is that you?"

My heart continues to pound as I follow Stone back, past the big, open chef's kitchen and into the den.

There Bonnie is, curled up on the couch, blankets tucked around her like she's a baby bird in a nest. She doesn't look much bigger than one. Bonnie was always gorgeous—a voluptuous woman with big hips and piles of black hair on her head. It makes me happy that despite her new birdlike frame she doesn't seem to have lost her hair.

"Hi, Bonnie," I say. "It's Lauren Novak."

Her face changes from slight confusion into recognition, and she breaks into a smile.

"Sweetheart," she says. "It's so good to see you."

Stone sits down next to her and takes her hand. The easy, gentle way he touches her.

"Here," she says. "Sit."

She makes an effort to move over.

"No no, stay," I say. I slip down next to Stone. "It's really good to see you."

Her eyes are a deep brown, and her skin is still covered in freckles. I look at Stone next to her—they could not possibly look less alike. Of course they're not related, not genetically, anyway. But the love between them is so evident here.

I remember now, sitting with Bonnie, a conversation we had out on the deck, right before Stone left for Colorado. I asked her if she'd ever wanted children of her own.

"We tried," she told me. "For a few years. But I was older when

I met Jeff, and it just didn't happen. And I knew what I had in Stone. He's been my son since the day I met him."

I didn't ask whether she pursued fertility treatment—I wouldn't have known what it was back then. I'd never even heard the word. But I remember her clarity. I've thought about it a lot these past three years.

When Leo and I first decided we wanted a child it felt like playing hooky. That first time we didn't use protection, the first time we "tried"—it felt like we'd never been together before that. Everything was new and exciting and innocent, in a way. It felt like the beginning—not even of our relationship, but of our sexual selves. It felt like being a teenager, discovering our bodies for the very first time.

I kept expecting my desire for this child, this baby, to wane. With every passing cycle, every failed IVF, I kept feeling like I'd come around to Leo's point of view. That I'd see the cost of this, all of it, and I'd decide to prioritize something else, the things that are actually here. That I'd want to jet off to Spain, or retile the bathroom. Give up and get on with it.

But that moment never came.

"Tell me," Bonnie says. She closes her eyes briefly. I see the translucent skin stretched across the backs of her lids. "What are you reading?"

Stone looks at me. His face is smiling. Even his eyes. "Some things never change."

Bonnie nudges him softly with her hand.

I am happy to be able to report something I know she will like. "I just finished *Sylvia's Second Act* by Hillary Yablon and I really loved it."

Bonnie closes her eyes again. She rests her head on the wall behind the couch. "Tell me what it's about."

I look at Stone. He nods.

"A woman in her sixties finds out her husband is cheating on her and leaves their Florida retirement home to restart her life in New York."

Bonnie smiles. "Some inspiration."

"Jeff would never," I say—half kidding, really, because of course.

"No," Bonnie says, suddenly earnest. "He wouldn't."

I see Jeff and Bonnie—healthy, vivacious, young—in the kitchen. His arms around her waist, kissing the crook of her neck. I remember them dancing to Rod Stewart and Van Morrison. "Crazy Love" drifting through the sound system.

"I always remember you as being so in love," I say, because it feels important to tell her. I want her to know. "It's always been so clear to me how much Jeff adores you."

"Thank you," she says. "You knew us in the glory days."

"Still good ones ahead," Stone says. He kisses the side of her face.

I see a tear escape down her cheek. I should feel like an intruder. I should excuse myself, let Bonnie rest, let her be with her son. But I don't. Instead, I press my fingers into Bonnie's open palm. I feel her hand close around mine.

"I'm glad I'm here," I say.

She opens her eyes, and when she looks at me it's like no time has passed. I'm seventeen again, back in her living room being handed a bowl of popcorn.

"Me, too," she says.

CHAPTER FOURTEEN

No one knows where Sylvia's money comes from. Not my mother, who grew up here. Not my father, who has always been at least partially in charge of the finances of Broad Beach. Certainly not me.

"There's money," Sylvia says. "It's not yours, so don't worry about it."

My grandmother was always a riddle. Beginning with: Who was my grandfather? My mother tried to find him, I think, online—she didn't get very far.

"He left," Sylvia said. "That's all we need to know."

Sylvia wasn't cold about it, not exactly, although it couldn't have been easy for my mom anyway—to have such little information, to have a mother with such little interest in giving her any. But Sylvia was never very interested in the past, hers maybe especially. "Keep it moving, baby" was her favorite things to say.

I asked my mother about it once, and her response was vague. Something like "You can't miss what you don't know." But I knew she did, miss something—if not him than the idea of a nuclear family.

Marcella had met her own grandparents just three times in her life. Once when she was too little to remember.

"A practical woman," my mom once told me when I asked.

"My mother was not sentimental," Sylvia has said. "But she was from the Old World. No one had that luxury back then."

When I was growing up Sylvia would sometimes disappear for long stretches at a time, telling no one she was leaving or where she was going.

When she'd return I'd ask her, "G-money, where did you go?"

Her answers were always a skirt. "To a luxurious villa." Or: "Somewhere fabulous." Or: "My favorite city." Or: "To a really good time." No real explanation.

It bothered my mom. She wanted to know where Sylvia was, if she was safe, and, mostly, when she was coming home.

"It's not good for Lauren," my mom would say. "You act like there is no one relying on you here. You have a family."

Sylvia would always scoff. "She's not my daughter; she's yours. But if you're asking for my parenting advice, I think she could do with a little *less* stability."

In my early years I was in awe of Sylvia—she seemed to me less like a grandmother and more like a fairy godmother. Popping in and out, always in a cloud of mystique and expensive perfume, always with a treat or dress or doll. I looked forward to her leaving because I knew when she returned there would be something to celebrate. She was an apparition, an energy, the embodiment of everything Marcella wasn't.

As Sylvia got older we spiraled off in different directions—I moved out just as she started to stay closer to home. Over time Sylvia stopped traveling entirely.

"I've seen it all," she told me. "There's nothing more for me out there that isn't here."

I expected my mother to love this—it's what she always wanted:

Sylvia home, in her orbit day in and day out, finally. But instead of becoming closer over the years, they've grown more distant. They have dinners together but don't do much of anything else. At least, I don't hear about it.

After I leave Bonnie's I come home to an uncharacteristically busy house. Sylvia is doing tai chi with an instructor over Zoom, who blasts through the computer at a screech.

My dad is having breakfast in the kitchen, watching television at a volume that is clearly trying to compete with the living room sound, and my mom is banging around pots and pans, cleaning up the sink.

"Hello!" I holler, over the noise.

Sylvia gives me exaggerated, overhead waves. "Want to join?"

She's dressed in black leggings that buckle at the knees and an old T-shirt that has "Coors Cowboy" on it.

"Just ate," I say, "but keep crushing it." I flex my bicep at her, she flexes back.

"Honey!" Dave says. He immediately grabs the remote and turns down the TV volume. "How was the water?"

I flop my bag onto the counter and move to fill up a glass with water. "How did you know?"

Dad's cheeks go wide into a smile. "Just the look," he says. He takes a big bite of toast. "And also your board was gone."

Marcella turns around, a spatula in her hand. She's dressed in white linen pants and a blue-striped button-down. She looks like she just stepped out of a J.Crew catalog.

"Did you see Stone?" she says.

"Yeah." I gulp down some water. "We ended up going to the Cove for breakfast." I decide to leave out the part about Bonnie. I don't want them to ask me how she is. I don't want to have to tell them.

"I see him out there sometimes when he's back. Boy can shred. A lot like the old man," Dave says.

He grabs my mom's elbow and pulls her toward him. He kisses her, and I look, briefly, away.

"You don't need to be shredding," my mom says.

The tension between them about the water hasn't waned, but it's also the one area where my dad drew a line that Marcella doesn't totally cross. He's yielded to her on most areas of life and family and parenting, but on this one, Dave was the law: His daughter would surf; she would love the water. And he'd be in there with her.

"How is Stone?" Dad asks. "Still in Denver?"

"Boulder. He never got married," my mom says. "Jeff used to talk to me about it."

"How could you after this one?" Dad extends his arm toward me.

"Well," Marcella says. "Of course."

She looks at me and smiles slightly.

I don't want to talk about Stone, or Bonnie. And I realize how long it has been since I've spoken to my husband.

"I'm gonna head up; I need to do some work and call Leo."

"Send my love!" Dad says.

I hear Marcella cover a stainless steel pot with a clank.

I go into my bedroom, and before I unplug my phone from in the charger I go to the bathroom. I still have my period, and I'm bleeding this morning in spurts of crimson—a reinvigorated day four. I feel the grief settle around me—both at another failed attempt and at the unknown of the future—our fight, Leo's absence. But I notice, too, a thread of newfound freedom. Just a whisper, a small taste of it. If we do nothing, there will be nothing, but also: There's nothing I need to do.

In the beginning, fertility treatment felt like a necessary step, a means to an end. Productive, even. After a year of not getting pregnant, we were doing something to change that. OK, so we have to take Clomid; OK, so we have to do IUI; OK, so we have to do IVF. They were just the steps we had to take to become parents. I never considered the possibility that they wouldn't work. That nothing we did was going to bring us any closer. That, in fact, every month that went by made the possibility of our success bleaker and bleaker.

I've never been pregnant, but I have once seen double lines on a pregnancy test. About a year ago we did an IUI cycle that started as a potential IVF but not enough follicles grew—only one—and we pivoted to IUI. Less invasive but, more importantly, less expensive. I had done a myriad of shots, but we weren't going to go through the out-of-pocket surgical procedure. And the month wouldn't be a total waste. I knew it wasn't going to work, but also—fertility treatment leads to magical thinking. But, maybe, perhaps—everyone had an exception story.

We weren't supposed to test until day fourteen. Two weeks past procedure. Sometimes the trigger shot took a while to work its way out of your system—a week, ten days, tops. Two weeks was enough time for real pregnancy HCG to grow detectable in the body. Enough time to get a BFP (big fat positive). In the early days, before intervention, I became obsessed with testing. I'd test at day seven, day nine, holding the pink test strips up into the light and squinting. Did I see something? Maybe? No, just "line eyes." All the terminology poured out of other hopeful women on Reddit. I found myself part of the TTC community, when before I would have cringed at the acronym. That was me, trying to conceive.

Leo quickly told me we had to exhibit some self-restraint. "This is too much of a roller coaster," he'd say. "We'll test on day fourteen, until then, we live our lives."

The day came. I had been feeling unwell the past three days—unwelcome, normally, but in a pretest window, drenched in hope. Every wave of nausea or stuffed-up nose or abdominal twitch made me think maybe—just maybe—our luck was about to change.

I took the tests. Three of them, just to be sure. They were all positive.

I ran into the living room holding them up, screaming for Leo. "Look!" I said. "Do you see that?"

He did.

We cried; we held each other. We made plans to drive out to the beach that night. "We'll hand them one," I told Leo. "We'll wrap it up and hand it to them."

I saw my parents, tears in their eyes, a hand clamped over my mother's mouth.

They didn't know what we were going through—we hadn't shared. To them, it would all be upside, all joy.

"You're making me feel old!" Sylvia would say, throwing her arms around us. "A great-grandchild."

We held each other at the door. Leo was going to work—he was helping a director friend with some postproduction at a studio in Hollywood—and I was heading to the clinic to confirm the pregnancy with a blood test.

"Call me as soon as you hear," he said. He kissed me hard. "I love you so fucking much."

I had never walked in the doors to the clinic and had this reception before. All the nurses—Becky and Jaime and Tenacity and Shayanna—were beaming.

"We knew it!" they said. The relentless positivity of Reproductive had annoyed me in the past, it felt like a mosquito buzzing, but now I welcomed it. We *had* known, hadn't we?

I held up my crossed fingers to indicate *Not yet*, to say, *I am being cautious*, but it was just a front. I was already drunk on joy, already calculating a due date, letting the past two years fall away in a dissolve of *it was all worth it*.

And then the call came. In the middle of Party City. I was there buying tissue paper. In my hand was a full sheet of white and something yellow with pink flowers on it.

"This isn't a good call," Becky said. She didn't drag it out. "You're not pregnant."

Any line, however faint, meant positive. Any line. There had been two of them, three times over. "What do you mean?" I said.

I wanted it to be true so badly. I wanted to be pregnant even if it was a chemical pregnancy. I'd find myself jealous of women who had miscarriages. I longed to just know I could. To experience the beginning, even if it wouldn't last.

"The trigger shot must have lingered in your system a lot longer than it usually does. We don't see this often, but your HCG level is only 2.7. It would have to be over five to be a pregnancy. I am so sorry."

I wasn't pregnant. I'd never been pregnant. I just had some medication in my system, and probably indigestion.

I put the yellow paper back. I called Leo.

"Honey" was all I got out before I started crying.

"I'm on my way."

I beat him home, got in bed, and when I heard the door open, I remember feeling an overwhelming sense of guilt. That he didn't deserve this. That he thought he was having a baby and now he wasn't because of *my* body. Because of what it could not or refused to do.

That was the first time Leo expressed it, that maybe we were going too far.

"Are we sure?" he said, as we held each other. "I don't want you to go through this anymore."

"We have to," I said.

He didn't fight me on it, not yet—and that was over a year ago, now. And every month since we have carried on. The thing about infertility is the absolute idiocy of hope. The bottomless well of it. The way it refreshes and refreshes and refreshes. After every retrieval, after every failed phone call, after the comedown off the hormones and drugs there it is again. Waiting.

I blink back the memory as Leo answers the phone.

"Hey," he says. I can hear the flood of city sounds behind him. "We're reversing. I can't really talk."

"Oh, OK," I say. "How is it going?"

I hear his voice get distant. "I don't think we need it. Does lighting want it?" Then he's back. "Hey, babe, I'll call you later, OK?"

He doesn't wait for my answer before hanging up.

I take out my computer and go through my emails methodically. In fifteen minutes flat I've answered them all, plus attached two documents to our bookkeeper, Peter, and sent the requisite 1099s a client requested for two ill-advised part-time employees she definitely cannot afford.

The truth is, being a CPA is a little like being a teacher. Not in practice—we are not impacting the world, at least, not with any great significance—but they are alike in the schedule. There are crunch periods—finals, tax season, but the summer is mostly off.

Even Wagner doesn't really go into the office all that much from June to Labor Day. I like the cyclical nature of my job.

I can hear the house has quieted. I take my laptop back down with me, hoping the kitchen has cleared.

Only Marcella is in the living room. She's reading, which is unusual. She's never been a big reader. Dad puts away a book a week, easy. He loves thrillers and spy novels, has mainlined the entire Grisham catalog. My mom always says she prefers life to books. But here she is, curled up with a cup of coffee.

I tilt my head down to read the cover, and she closes it.

Gravity's Rainbow by Thomas Pynchon. Yikes.

"Any good?" I ask.

She looks at me, trying to decide. "It might be if I stick with it." She pauses. "I've read the same chapter four times."

My mother usually does not poke fun at herself. I find myself taking a seat down next to her.

"I don't blame you," I say. "I don't think I ever got through it, either. It doesn't seem very enjoyable."

She laughs lightly. "It's really not."

She sets the book on the coffee table and shifts her body toward me.

"Dad didn't surf this morning," I say. I'm surprised I'm still thinking about it. Or maybe her vulnerability has given me an opening to something else.

"He's fine," she says, because she knows where I'm going with this. "He comes and goes—he's not as militant as he used to be."

"Are you sure?" That's three days in a row, by my calculations, that he hasn't been near the water.

"Ask him to go out with you tomorrow," she says. "I'm sure he'd love that."

"I thought you hate when he surfs."

She looks up at me and exhales. "I'm learning."

My mother is not a particularly beautiful woman. Whatever that means. She's cute, yes, and puts herself together well, absolutely. But her features do not exactly hang together. Her hair is straw-colored and chin-length, her nose is small and wide, and her eyes are big and almost rectangular. Something about her always seems disjointed or effortful. I've always thought I took after her physically. A little awkward. But when she looks up at me now, I see something softer than I've ever seen before.

"You look nice," I tell her.

I want to say something else, something about parenthood, maybe. The impossibility of my own—to actually tell her now. The weight that I'm carrying. Or about marriage, Leo being gone, the hard truths of commitment. Or I want to ask: "Will I be happy without a child?"

She looks up at me curiously. "You hate the way I dress," she says.

I blink at her. "Who said that?"

She shrugs in a way that feels practiced. "I don't know. You make it clear."

"Mom," I say. "You're reaching. I just told you you look nice."

"Well," she says. "Thank you." She flips her book back open.

"I called over to Bonnie's," she says. "Stone answered. I invited him to dinner tonight, if that's OK."

"Did you speak to her?" I ask.

"No. Stone said she isn't really up for visitors right now."

She looks at me a beat longer. I can't tell if she's waiting for me to tell her something—about my life, about Stone, about visiting Bonnie earlier—*Does she know?* But also—why does she never ask? Why is it always on me to cough up information for her to get to peruse at her liking? Aren't mothers supposed to pry you open?

"Is he coming?" I ask.

"Yes."

And then, as if the conversation is complete, she resettles herself and turns the page.

CHAPTER FIFTEEN

In those early, timid years, she dreams of having a baby at the beach. She dreams of her daughter.

Marcella wants to walk the sand with her and show her the seashells—hunt for coral and beach glass among the broken fragments of stone. She figures eventually they'll move to town—somewhere central, where she can stroll the baby everywhere. Dress her up in a little outfit and carry her on her hip for the whole world to see. Take her to a coffee shop, browse at their local bookstore.

Her little best friend. Her mini me.

They get pregnant quickly, once they decide. They are living with Sylvia, saving money to move out on their own, but when she gets pregnant, it isn't even a question: They will stay. Marcella knows nothing about being a mother, and even though she doesn't believe Sylvia knows much more, moving out of her home feels unthinkable. They'll stay with her mother, they'll save money, and they'll have the baby there.

Sylvia has the top floor in those days, and Marcella and Dave the room that is still theirs today. There is no back house, not yet.

Dave and Sylvia get along—better, in many ways, than Sylvia and Marcella ever have. They don't have a history to contend with, to interrupt the harmony and flow of the present. Sylvia cooks, and Dave fixes things, and Marcella fills in the gaps—she buys paper towels and batteries and power-washes the deck when it needs it. She starts to make Malibu her adult home.

Lauren is born in the dead of winter, during one of the coldest Februarys Los Angeles has ever recorded. Marcella packs up a bunting for her—part puffer jacket, part hooded blanket. The baby spends four days in the hospital with jaundice and is returned to Marcella's arms looking pink and perfect.

"Lauren," Marcella says, without consulting anyone, not even Dave. "My baby's name is Lauren."

She loves the name, always has. It reminds her of normalcy and femininity—but still hearty. She cringes at the popular names surrounding her—Bethany and Tiffany. They all sound like accessories stores, but not Lauren. Lauren is dignified.

Sylvia visits in the hospital. She is uncharacteristically doting—asking Marcella what she needs, smoothing her hair down. Marcella cannot remember a time, except for early childhood, when they got along better, and she finds herself caught between affection at the possibility that Sylvia is recalling her own tender, lonely days of early motherhood, and jealousy that her new baby has been able to elicit this reaction from her mother.

They never speak about Marcella's father, not because it's a sore subject but because there isn't much to say. There was no email back then, no iPhone, no way to trace and link every encounter.

To her knowledge Sylvia has never regretted the affair that led to Marcella, and Marcella, for all her issues with Sylvia, has not missed having a father as much as one might think.

It isn't until Lauren is born that Marcella begins to long for a dad—not for herself, at least, not entirely, but for her child. She wants Lauren to have a full and complete family. A grandfather to toss her in the air, sing to her, have her nap on his big, wide chest. She doesn't say this to Sylvia, but she tells Dave, late one night in the hospital room, when it's just the two of them—the baby napping in the nursery down the hall.

"Do you think I should try to find my father?" she asks him.

He is perched on her hospital bed, and he touches her cheek. "Is that what you want?"

She nods.

"Then we'll do it."

But they don't, because she doesn't remember. Such are the demands of new motherhood. They bring the baby home to a house full of balloons and flowers. Sylvia has stocked the fridge with food. She's in the kitchen wearing a "Kiss the Grandma" apron when they arrive. She sets out salads and egg sandwiches, and Dave makes them all plates while Marcella takes Lauren outside.

Marcella holds the baby to her chest, and the little one curls up, as if trying to burrow back under her skin.

"You smell that?" she tells her. "This is the beach."

Marcella does not find new motherhood hard, only challenging. The way a nice long run is after a day on a plane. She feels energized, activated—fulfilled for the first time in her life. This is where she belongs. Here, with her child.

Dave goes back to work quickly, but Marcella doesn't miss him as much as she thought she might. Even after the first few months, when Sylvia begins to dip back into her old life, starts traveling again, Marcella isn't lonely. She doesn't need anyone but Lauren.

But when Sylvia is in town Marcella tries to include her in their unit—make it a threesome.

"Come with us," she tells her mother.

They leave their shoes at the door and take buckets down to the beach. As Lauren gets older she hunts for treasure by the shore. Marcella cannot imagine anything better than this—her mother and her daughter and the edge of the ocean.

"She's spunky," Sylvia tells her. "She's going to be a little wild, just like her G-money," she says. Sylvia had named herself that, refusing to be called "Grandma."

"She can be whatever she wants to be," Marcella says, and she means it.

And sure enough, as Lauren grows so does her spirit. But it's not just in size, it's in direction. It grows away from Marcella.

Lauren is adventurous. She no longer wants to pick up shells with a shovel but instead wants to lay on a slab of foam and dive headfirst into waves with her father. She wants to run—faster, farther than Marcella is capable of. Lauren begins to leave her.

It happens slowly, but it doesn't feel that way, not at all. One day she is flying down the stairs, right into Marcella's arms, and the next she is stealing the car keys, the Scotch, rolling her eyes at everything her mother wears and says and does. One day she is sneaking out into the water before Marcella is even conscious.

"Oh, you did the same thing," Sylvia says. "Give her some space."

But Marcella never rebelled, she never wanted to move away from Sylvia—in fact, she was always desperate for her. It was Sylvia who didn't need Marcella. And now, neither does Lauren.

Sometimes Marcella blames Sylvia for turning her daughter against her, although she knows this is not fair. If anyone is responsible for Lauren's spirit, it is Dave.

Everything that proves her daughter's independence takes her outside the house, and everything that proves Marcella's keeps her inside it, because what does she have if not this family? If not this marriage?

Dave has always been her solace—she knew when she met him that they would be married, and she knew after they were married that it would last. He is a kind man, yes, but more than that, he takes her side. *Happy wife, happy life*, the old adage goes. She has found it has the benefit of being true.

"Whatever you think, sweetheart," he says often, and she knows he's not trying to appease her. That just like she married him for his foundation, he married her for her conviction. He trusts her judgment.

He trusts her judgment with his supplements—the vitamin D, the zinc, the B12 shots he gets monthly, on her orders. He trusts it with her design sense, the way she decorates their home: the new pillows she buys for their bed, the lamps for the living room. He trusts her with vacations, the small trips she books—Catalina for the weekend, Cabo for spring break. The only area he has ever pushed back on is Lauren—specifically, the risks he's willing for her to take physically.

Dave pushes her into waves; he hikes with her on mountains; he convinces Marcella they should buy her a surfboard for her seventh birthday.

"She's too young," Marcella says.

"She's ready," Dave tells her.

He's adamant about this. He wants Lauren to experience the thrill of life. And Marcella trusts him, doesn't she? She tries to trust him. As Lauren grows and the two of them experience a water language all their own, Marcella has no choice but to.

It isn't until the accident that things start to change. That she sees a hint of her worry burrow down into Lauren—and remain. At first she is breathless with guilt, but over time that changes into something else. Because now, at last, Lauren has something in common with her mother.

CHAPTER SIXTEEN

Stone arrives at 7:00 p.m. on the dot, carrying a bottle of Sancerre and a bushel of sunflowers, cut from Bonnie's deck. He's dressed in jeans and a Hawaiian-print shirt that looks faded and thrifted but is probably closer to brand-new and three hundred dollars.

"Hey," he says when I answer the door. His hand is suspended, fist closed. "I'm actually not sure I've ever knocked before."

I'm wearing a blue-and-gray-striped knit sweater over a white sundress that I realized too late looks like a nightgown. It's warm out, but the ocean breeze is starting to cool everything down.

"Come in," I say. "I don't think the house looks that much different."

It's true—neither Marcella nor Sylvia has done much redecorating in the past decade.

Stone steps inside gingerly, like he's entering a dimension where the floor is just a little bit breakable. "Place looks great," he says.

"Stone, honey." Marcella comes into the entryway and gives him a hug. He hands her over the wine.

"Thank you, sweetheart," my mother says to him, then to me: "Your dad's out back. Go ahead and I'll open this."

She taps the wine with her index finger.

Stone follows me through the kitchen. Sylvia is making fish in parchment. Something white—maybe cod or branzino—with grape tomatoes, olive oil, lemon slices, and olives.

Stone comes up behind her and grabs her gently around the waist. She smiles into him.

"Hello there," Sylvia says. "Still single?"

"Why, you know anyone?"

Sylvia looks him up and down. "Me."

Stone laughs. His laugh was always loud, open, unapologetic. He laughs like someone who has never worked in an office before. "You're too good for me, and you know it."

Sylvia pins the parchment with a toothpick. "I'd settle."

I see Dad through the glass, and he waves us outside. Stone holds the slider open for me.

There's a bottle of red open on the railing and two small water glasses. I gesture to Stone, he nods, and I pour.

Dad offers Stone his hand from the chair, shakes it. "How you been?"

"Not bad," Stone says. "Happy to be back in the water."

"I hear you're here under hard circumstances." He gestures with his head in the direction of Stone's home. "I'm sorry. We're thinking about Bonnie over here."

Stone nods, sips. "Yeah, thank you."

The truth is, I'm not sure Dad ever really liked Stone. Part of it I think was that Stone was rich and Dad was not. Or Stone was a better surfer. Or he didn't like the way Jeff treated the beach like company stock. But part of it was that Stone always struck my dad as living too easily.

"You want a life where you can feel the road underneath you," Dad used to tell me. "You want a life with some traction."

I wonder, now, watching the two of them together, if Stone ever knew. We didn't talk about it—we were too young then. I'd have told him flippantly, a joke—*You know my dad thinks you're spoiled*—or not at all. I chose not at all.

Marcella comes out with the white wine. "Oh, you started." She sets the bottle down on the coffee table. It clinks against the glass.

I feel a pang of irritation—she's the one who told us to come out.

"Thanks so much for having me," Stone says. "It's really nice to see you guys. It's nice to be back here."

I consider our graying deck, the splintered wood on the banister. Still the best view on Broad Beach.

Stone looks my mom in the eye. I am reminded of his eye contact, the way he used to look at me, hold my gaze. I was fifteen when Stone and I first kissed, sixteen when we had sex for the first time. In so many ways Stone was not only my first love but also my orientation to men in general. He was the placeholder. For years afterward, whenever I'd meet a new man I'd compare him to Stone. How he stood, how he talked, how he kissed. I could see if the guy was right for me by judging how closely he aligned with Stone.

Leo was the first man I met whose metric had nothing to do with Stone. I couldn't have measured them on the same scale—it would have been like weighing air and fire.

"I think we're about ready to eat," Marcella says.

Stone rubs his hands together in a way that makes it seem like he hasn't had a home-cooked meal in quite some time. "Starving," he says. "I've missed Sylvia's cooking."

We file inside. Mom has set the table, and Sylvia is putting down the salad. Dark leaves of spinach curled underneath piles of shaved Parmesan.

"White fish—Mediterranean style—salad, and some rice," Sylvia says. She takes a seat, starts helping herself. "Everyone eat."

Stone holds my chair out for me, and I sit. He follows down next to me.

"I hear great things about the Ranch," Dad says. "Still haven't been to check it out, though. Damn it's pricey."

"I'm happy to hook you up," Stone says. "Any time."

"I do OK on the real ocean."

Stone just smiles. "Of course," he says.

Stone was always a humble person, but he also knew the way he appeared to other people. He was aware that every girl at Malibu High wanted him, and he'd remind me of it, sometimes, in ways he thought were subtle but weren't.

But now I see the ways he has softened. His privilege isn't something he carries around proudly anymore but something he wears. Like a leather jacket that has become supple with age.

"Well, I'd love to check it out," Marcella says. "Maybe I'd actually get in the water if it wasn't the real ocean. Do you temperature control?"

Stone laughs. "Just say the word and I will make it happen."

I serve myself some fish. It's flaky, salty, perfect. The tomatoes are sweet, the olives soft and juicy.

"This is delicious," Stone says. "Thank you."

Sylvia nods. "Happy to have you at the table," she says.

I know Sylvia always liked Stone, but she loves Leo, too. If I asked Sylvia who she enjoyed more, she'd probably say something like: *Why choose? Can't I have them both?*

Stone pours more wine for me. I drink much less than I used to, partially because my hangovers got exponentially worse on the other side of thirty-five and partially because for the past three years I have been maybe-pregnant. People are always saying that you can't be just "a little bit" pregnant, but those people have never done repetitive fertility treatment. I'm a little bit pregnant all the time.

But not today.

I take a long sip and feel my stomach get liquid and warm.

Marcella lowers her voice. "It was good to see Bonnie last week," she says. "She looked well."

I think about the woman we saw—curled up on the couch, barely bigger than the blanket covering her. A hot rod of anger pinches my stomach. No, actually, she does not *look well*.

Stone shakes his head. "She doesn't," he says. "But thanks for saying."

My mom opens her mouth and then closes it again.

"Will you hand me the bread?" Sylvia says.

Stone obliges at the same time my dad reaches for the water pitcher. Their hands collide, and the water pitcher spills, pouring all over dad, before falling to the ground and shattering.

Immediately, Marcella springs into action. "Honey," she says. "Hang on. Hold on. Don't stand up!"

I see her run into the kitchen. She grabs one of the dish towels that are flung over the lip of the sink and runs back. She starts with his pants, flicking off dollops of water.

"Marcie, honey, I'm fine. I'm fine."

"Hold still. Here. There could be glass."

Dad sits there, his hands at his sides, as my mother gets on her hands and knees and begins to pick up the shards from the floor.

"Marcella, please, let me help." Stone is out of his chair and crouching down next to her.

"Please just get a trash bag," she tells him.

Stone looks to me and I stand, too, and we go into the kitchen.

"Under the sink," I say.

He ducks and recovers one. We look back at the table. Sylvia, who has never once put down her fork, is eating happily. My parents are still caught in their hysteria dance. My mom bends on the floor, collecting glass shards in the palm of her hand. She looks up when Stone hands her the bag.

"Thanks."

Stone returns to me. "When will she learn it's just water?" he says.

I realize I'm not embarrassed, not even a little. Because Stone knows. He knows my parents, he knows their dance, the way in which they orbit each other. Once, in the eleventh grade, my mother missed volleyball playoffs because she was taking my dad to a dentist appointment.

I remember thinking there was nothing strange with this until Stone said it: "Why?"

Because that's who my parents are; they do everything together. Because that's who my mom is, terrified. And it was the worst in those early years—right after the accident, right when Stone and I got together. He was there for the crux of it, and I was too young and shell-shocked myself to protect him from anything. I didn't shield him, and so he saw it all. He saw the mess and the terror and the precarious way we were a family, defined by our reactions to one another. My mother's fear of losing my father, my father's fear of upsetting her.

Tonight, standing with Stone in the kitchen, watching my mother pick up glass like it's radioactive, like it could kill my father, like maybe, actually, it is—feels like a kind of relief I didn't know I needed. Because he sees it, too. I'm not alone in it; he's standing right here, witnessing.

I protect Leo, I think. And I hide it, too—my own fear, my mother's—in ways I never thought to when I was with Stone. Here he is, seeing it all—and none of it is a surprise to him. None of it is making him turn away.

"Watch your thumb!" Marcella says.

I feel Stone's hand on my hip. It's gentle, brief, merely a tap. I look to him and he swipes Sylvia's cooking wine off the counter.

"Let's go," he says, cocking his head toward the kitchen door.

It's not locked, still open from our time outside, and it swings easily and without noise. In high school when we didn't want to wake anyone, we'd sneak out through it. It was as good to us then as it is now.

Outside, the night is cold. Stone grabs a hoodie off the outdoor chair where it's been siting since I left it last night—and hands it to me. When you live at the beach there is almost always a stray sweatshirt outside. This one is surprisingly dry.

I gesture to my sweater, already on. "You take it," I say.

He loops his arms through the sleeves—it's small on him, but not by much.

"Come on," he says. He cuffs his pants at the ankle, and we take the steps down to the ocean. The sand is wet and dense, and there isn't much beach. The tide is high, just a sliver remains to walk down.

I know before he holds out his hand where we're going to

go. The Greek. A dilapidated, crumbling, splinter-filled house that has never been sold or occupied. At least not in the twenty years since we first went there. It's about half a football field down the beach, sandwiched between a blue-and-white beach house owned by the founders of that popular diaper company and the rocks.

Everyone on Broad Beach knew that's where kids went to party. Parents liked it because at least we were close by and accessible. If it was past midnight, they knew where to find us. But for us—we thought we were pulling off something major.

The house was already named long before Stone and I ever entered high school. The Greek, after a frat house, a meeting place, somewhere with sticky, beer-stained floors and broken glass windows. It had all of those things.

There were old, wooden steps up to the back deck that didn't quite reach the shore. Even when we were kids we'd have to leap up onto the first one and climb from there. It made the whole thing feel even more special, isolated—you had to work to get there.

"Wow," I say when we reach it. "It looks even worse, if that's possible."

Stone laughs lightly beside me.

"You think teenagers still come here?"

"Not anymore," he says. "They just party in their houses now. Parents are cooler. Or they care less than they used to."

I remember Bonnie offering us wine with dinner. *If you're going to drink I'd rather you do it here.*

"Yours didn't," I say.

I can't see Stone's face as he hops up onto the first step and offers me his hand. "Watch the wood," he says. He points to where it's splintered.

"Sorry. I shouldn't have said that." I push off the sand, and then grip his hand to steady myself.

"Why?"

"I don't know," I say truthfully. "I don't know how to talk about Bonnie."

We climb the remaining stairs, and then we're on the deck. It's black and green with mold and white with age. The spots sing out, iridescent in the dark night.

"We don't have to," Stone says. "Seriously, I'd rather not tonight. There's plenty else to say."

I look through the broken glass windows inside. There's no furniture—there never was. Although at one point a kid brought an old abandoned mattress over. That's long since decomposed.

Moss grows over the countertops and the floorboards.

"We're probably better off outside," I say. "I care more about asbestos than I used to."

"I really can't say the same."

Stone holds my gaze for a moment. It's dark out here, but the moon is near full, and its reflection off the water offers just enough light to see everything I need to.

I take a seat at the edge of the deck and dangle my feet off the side. Stone folds himself down beside me.

I'm thinking, now, about my twenty-third birthday. How he'd taken me to Duke's on the water for fish tacos and then blindfolded me in the car. He'd driven me back to this house, but before we got there we pulled into the parking lot at the Trancas shopping center. It's where we had gone in high school when we needed somewhere we could be alone together. When our busy houses were bustling and the doors to both our bedrooms had to be open.

I remember the way the leather of his back seat felt against my skin, how he lay my body over the arm rest. I remember the windows fogging to a tilt, the beads of sweat on his forehead, the way he'd drawn slow and lazy circles until I was breaking. For years I couldn't drive by that corner of PCH without a sting of memories. Our parking lot. Sometimes it felt like we were still there.

I remember, now, how much I used to want. How impossible it felt to be apart from him, even for a day. How I'd lose whole nights to not even his body but the idea of it. How I'd fall asleep imagining his mouth on mine. For years after—past thirty, even, if I'm honest—whenever I couldn't sleep I'd think of us in bed together. I'd imagine his arms around me, and I'd drift off.

Stone elbows me lightly, interrupting the memory. "So how are you?" he says. "Really?"

I think about the question. How am I? Really? The IVF bills, the hovering of infertility, the job that has long since plateaued. But it feels cruel, somehow, to say it out loud. Although to him or to me or to Leo, I'm not sure.

"Fine," I say. "You know."

"I don't," he says. "That's why I'm asking."

"Life," I say. I shrug. "It gets more complicated, doesn't it?"

Stone appears to really consider this. "I don't know," he says. "Maybe we make it more complicated."

I think about Bonnie. "But look at what's happening in your family."

"What's happening is very real. But real and complicated are not the same thing." He sits up and brushes his palms against each other. "Actually, I'd argue that impending death makes everything really simple."

It's the first time we've said it: *death*. The reality of why he's here. An inevitability.

"It's the biggest thing there is," I say.

I remember that night like a trauma. How after my mother and grandmother told me about what had happened to my father I'd gone to Stone's. We had just gotten together, but we were fifteen. We didn't need help figuring out how to blur the lines between friend and more. Our bodies knew for us.

"What happened?" he'd asked me. He was wearing a striped shirt and board shorts. He was always in board shorts back then. Always slightly wet from the water.

I hadn't told him. I hadn't known how. But I had folded to him in the way you can only do when you're very young—when you believe other people have the power to save you, to make the world whole again. He had wrapped his arms around me in response to the question I hadn't answered. And it was enough. Somehow, then, it was enough.

Stone doesn't say anything right away, now. He just keeps looking at me.

"I don't know," he says, either to save himself or me. "But there are times when I think about it, and I wonder if I fucked it all up."

I feel my heartbeat begin to drum. *Thump thump thump.* "What?"

"I moved, why did I move? I missed a decade with Bonnie, with the ocean." He looks up at me, and I silently ask him not to say it. He doesn't. Instead, he just shakes his head. "There are so many things I'd do differently."

I think about how easy it would be, to turn back the clock. To go back to twenty-five. To tell him not to go. To demand it. Would it make a difference?

It wasn't what I wanted then, was it?

"You're happy," he says. "I'm not."

"I can't have a baby."

The words tumble out. Whether they're to make him feel better or because they are the truth, I don't know. I've avoided putting our "situation" into such concise verbiage. There is a multibillion-dollar industry around fertility that tells you to Speak It Into Existence that tells you your Words Have Power and Nothing Is Impossible. It says Pay Us and you'll get knocked up, and then when you don't, it says You're Just Too Stressed—here, relax, have some lavender. Have you tried these herbs? That'll be twenty thousand, please. And don't forget: *It's all up to you*. Which really means: *It's all your fault*.

On the rotted wood deck of the Greek, Stone takes my hand. We sit that way, side by side, listening to the waves of the ocean as if the water has the answers.

CHAPTER SEVENTEEN

Dave has open-heart surgery the summer before Lauren starts the second grade. He needs three bypasses and an aortic valve replacement. Marcella is stupefied. They are so young! Not even forty! What has happened?

He has coronary artery disease. They discover this after an episode walking up the beach steps. Dave feels the sudden constriction, falls to his knees.

They are lucky they caught it when they did, the doctors say. Another few days and he'd be dead. Surgery will help for a long time—decades, perhaps—but it, like all human things, is not a permanent solve.

Marcella is woefully unprepared for this twist, this knot in the thread of her life. She has a curious young daughter who spends most of her time in the water, and a mother who has just built herself a back house and has no plans on leaving. They are trying to navigate three generations in the same household, and Dave, in many ways, is the lubricant that makes it all turn.

In the hospital Marcella is measured and stoic. Dave's parents fly in from New York—big, lively, Upper West Siders who bring bagels into the waiting room and hug Marcella as if it's her wedding, not this.

"Susan and Mitch are the best!" Sylvia says, raising a Styrofoam coffee cup next to a young mother sitting with a crying baby on her lap.

Marcella feels anger coil in her stomach. Sylvia cannot understand because she's never had a partner, never felt the weight and responsibility of joining your life with someone else's. The casualness with which Sylvia moves through life, the ease with which she encounters tragedy, leaves Marcella breathless. She has no choice but to assume it just means her mother does not care.

In the prep room before surgery Marcella holds tightly to Dave's hand.

"I'm more worried about your grip than this operation!" he jokes.

He is doing it for her, of course, because he sees the fear in her eyes and feels it in her hands. That is who Dave is—her stabilizer. He sees her, in a way no one ever has—not her mother, not her daughter, not her friends, the few she has maintained. He is her focus. If he goes, she fears in a way—in all the ones that matter—so will she. She has never considered the possibility that this might end. Motherhood did not make her confront mortality. It's here now, holding on to her husband's hand, and she is met with the reality that no one lives forever.

The doctor comes in. His bedside manner leaves something to be desired, but Marcella appreciates his fact-driven preamble. He tells them how long it will last (six hours) and how complicated it will be (fairly). He is confident, and Marcella trusts him, because he does not smile.

"I love you," she tells Dave. They have never held back in saying it. She is grateful for that now, all the easy love they have always allowed themselves to express.

"I love you, too, honey. Walk in the park."

He kisses her hand, although it is a struggle with all the tubing, and they wheel him away. Susan and Mitch have left to look after Lauren, but Sylvia is there, in that waiting room, when Marcella returns.

"They took him," Marcella says.

Sylvia nods.

"The doctor said a member of his team will keep us informed."

Sylvia exhales. She holds up a sweater. "Put this on," she says. "It's cold in here."

It is a level of maternal Marcella hasn't felt in so long, and she plucks the soft wool out of Sylvia's hands and threads her arms through the sleeves. It's big on her—it's Sylvia's—and it smells like her. Marcella breathes in.

"He's going to be all right," Sylvia says. "You just have to believe it. OK?"

Marcella nods. "OK."

Later, after the accident, in the same hospital on a different floor, Marcella will recall this moment with her mother. She will battle between anger that Sylvia did not offer the ticket then, that she watched her daughter in agony and said nothing—and gratitude that Marcella hadn't yet spent it. That in that moment her mother was, in a way, looking out for her.

Dave's recovery is challenging; it takes him a while to regain his appetite. He gets a viral infection—something lung-related—and ends back up in the hospital. But he is young—they both are—and while not linear, his recovery is expected. By her, by the doctors, and by him. They walk steadily toward it the way you walk toward home, knowing it's there. And little by little, it is granted to them.

When Dave goes into the water for the first time—five months after the surgery—Marcella has to sit on her hands to not say anything. She doesn't want to be a wife who nags—and the doctors say he is ready—but *she* is not.

She has, in a way, enjoyed this time even while longing for him to be better. She has enjoyed the way he has relied on her, how needed she has been. And now there her husband is, carrying his board down to the sand. Somewhere she can't follow.

"Be careful!" she calls, but he doesn't hear. It's too windy outside.

Dave isn't out long—maybe forty minutes—and when he comes inside, wet and smiling, she is ready with a towel. She dries him off and then makes him get directly into a hot shower.

"Your lungs," she says, and he lumbers toward the stairs.

And that's how it has stayed, more or less, for the duration of their marriage. She knows it only takes three weeks to form a habit, but she never wonders if her concern is a habit—it never even enters her mind. She just believes it is, like all things that are hidden. True. She has saved his life—over and over again. This is the beginning of that story.

CHAPTER EIGHTEEN

One week turns into two and then three, and by the time the rent check comes from West Hollywood, it's been almost a month since I've been at the beach. A full four weeks of waking up at the ocean. Of dinners with my family. Of Stone and I falling back in a surf rhythm.

Most mornings we meet down on the sand before the sun is up. If one of us doesn't show, the other will paddle out, and sometimes we find each other on the water.

I'm not back where I used to be, and I wouldn't say surfing is like riding a bike, not exactly, but there's a particular memory even if it isn't necessarily a muscle one. It's a mental memory, maybe even an energetic memory. The more I'm out on the water the more I begin to understand it, to anticipate it, to fall in line with it. It feels so good to be back in its good graces.

Respect her and she'll reward you, I remember my dad saying about the ocean. It's true.

Leo is busy in New York, and phone time is hard to come by. It's been over a week since I've heard his voice, and I miss it, I miss him. I knew when I married him he wasn't great with his cell, but living apart right now I feel his shortcoming in this area much more acutely. I try him when I wake up, but he's already setting up for the day, and by the end of their shoot day I know he's absolutely beat. If he calls and I miss him, he's usually asleep by the time I try him back.

This morning I call him at five, hoping to get a quick pickup, but instead I get his voicemail. I hang up, resigned, and then go out on dawn patrol. Stone isn't on the sand, and I paddle out alone, until I reach Kai, who is holding down the lineup without Bert.

The conditions aren't great—a lot of chop from crosswinds. And the waves aren't breaking cleanly. Kai gives up after a few sets. I follow suit.

I drag my board onto the sand and sit down next to it. I drape my forearms on my knees and look out over the water. The sun has risen, but the day is still new, quiet and sleepy.

When I think about having a child I often think about mornings here. It started far before I had gotten back in the water, before this month. For the past few years, really, I'd think about putting the baby on the board and pushing her into the spray. I'd think about dunking her head under and watching her eyes blink open, her mouth peel into a curl of salted smile. I'd think about watching her fall in love with the water, just like I did. It was as if I knew she would return me here, to this place I had long since left.

Leo and I were married here, right on the deck at sunset. It was beautiful and casual. I wore a white silk slip dress, and we decorated the house with wildflowers and roses from the garden. I wore a wreath of gardenias in my hair that yellowed by the time we said "I do" but smelled like heaven all night.

The beach was also the place we got engaged. Leo had planned a dinner for us in Hollywood, at a hotel called the Cara that has a beautiful outdoor restaurant situated around a pool. And then I got food poisoning. We had eaten some ill-advised supermarket sushi for lunch at the beach. Leo was fine, but I was, mysteriously, not. I've always had a strong stomach and can count on one hand how many times I've been sick—including frat parties in college. This time was poison.

After waves and waves of nausea—and hours of my life—it was finally over, and so was the day. I was lying on the bathroom floor when Leo brought me in another round of some Gatorade ice chips.

"I'm sorry about dinner," I said. Even the word *dinner* made my stomach turn, but I knew what he was going to do—trying to do—and I felt bad about ruining his plan. I didn't have the wherewithal to try to hide that from him.

"What could be more romantic than cold, hard ceramic tile?" he said.

I picked up my head. He knelt down on both knees. He tucked some hair behind my ear.

"What do you think?" he asked. "Should I do it?"

Up until that point I wasn't sure that he was aware that I knew, and I felt a rush of adrenaline that made me sit straight up. *This is really happening.*

"It would be a very good story," I said.

He smiled. He took my hand.

"Lauren Sylvester Novak."

"That's not my middle name."

"Shh," he said. "Let me have this one."

I squeezed his hand. We looked at each other. I felt all at once perfectly still. Like the volume had just been turned down on the whole rest of the world.

"I love you. I have loved you since you took me into your

world and made me feel like I was—am—worthy of being here. I've never had this. The way you care about me. There's nothing I won't do for you."

I started to cry. He already was.

"Will you marry me?"

I never even got the yes out. I never answered him. We were just hugging and kissing, falling into each other in a mix of devotion and dehydration.

Leo is a simple man. He likes good food and easy music and a stretch of uninterrupted time to putter around the house. He gave me a ruby-and-diamond band that was a little bit too big and took us forever to get resized. I loved it.

Afterward we went downstairs and told my parents.

"I thought you were going to do it at dinner?" my mother said.

"Things don't always go according to plan," Leo said, and the ease with which he said it, the way he embodied it, made me love him even more.

"Welcome to the family," my dad said. "I've been waiting a long time to get a little solidarity."

Sylvia simply took us both in her arms. "Couldn't be happier," she said. "Now, Leo, I have a sink that is leaking and no one around here is handy."

Leo looped his arm through Sylvia's and followed her into the kitchen. My mother went to chill some prosecco.

"So there we go," Dad said. He stood next to me as we watched Leo crouch down under the sink, trade Sylvia a screwdriver for a wrench.

"Yeah," I said. "There we go."

Marcella closed the refrigerator. "Do you need some paper towels?"

I felt all at once a very particular sadness that I couldn't quite identify until sometime later. For Leo my parents were in their third act. They were my parents. They were aging. They forgot things, were weaker in their bodies, didn't always understand the rhythm of modern life.

They weren't the nimble, athletic people I had known as a child. Dave didn't run the beach anymore; Marcella didn't plan spontaneous weekends away. They were set in their life, dug in, and I felt a pang of grief that Leo wouldn't share my memories. That in twenty years I wouldn't be able to roll over, look into his eyes, and say "Remember when Dad..."

There is a particular loneliness to being an only child. I never felt it as acutely as I did the day I decided to marry.

Leo wasn't close with his family, and I knew for him that there was no inherent or assumed responsibility. He had left home quite young, so had his siblings, and had been on his own from that point onward. He was used to being a one-man show, and I wondered how he would deal with the fact that I wasn't.

Now, I put my board away and hop in the shower. I'm supposed to go with Marcella to see Bonnie today, but Stone asked us to check in first on how she is. I've seen her only once in the month since my first visit, and it's like she's being erased before my eyes. Stone says he thinks the end is near, but she keeps holding on. I know how much Marcella wants to go today. I told Stone we'd call after eight.

I turn the water to a cold blast at the end and then step out, and as I'm toweling off I hear some commotion downstairs. I slip my robe around me and walk down to find Dad fumbling on the deck with his board. He's trying to flip it over, but he's having a hard time lifting it.

I watch him for a moment, caught between the desire to rush out and help him and the need to observe him to see what, exactly, age is doing to him. And as I watch him I have a feeling of perversion, something close to disgust, that creeps into the corners. Because he's Dave Novak, lifelong surfer, bulldog of a dad. And right now, he can't lift his board.

I am used to worrying about him, but I have very little practice with the worry being founded. It was all theoretical, wasn't it? A hidden heart condition, a deadly crash—neither of which we could actually see. But now, here, his limitations are on display.

He spots me before I make myself known. I see it dawn on him, this witnessing, and then he sighs, and lifts his hand in a wave. I open the door and go outside.

"How long?" I ask him.

He exhales. "Don't be so dramatic. Sometimes the old girl is heavier than she used to be."

"Why didn't you say anything?"

"What is there to say? I'm getting older."

"Does Mom know?"

"That I'm seventy-three? Yes, I think she does."

Dad smiles a big, goofy grin, and I feel my arms begin to slacken where they're crossed. It's funny how the first response to fear is often anger.

"Come on," he says, "sit down with me."

Dad gestures to the edge of the deck. I sit. So does he.

"I've started getting a little angina," he says. Casually, so casually. Like he's remarking on the surf conditions.

I turn to look at him but say nothing.

"Nothing significant. Just a little short of breath lately. I knew it would happen sooner or later."

"How long has it been going on?"

"Oh, who knows. You get older, things present. Nothing is a big deal."

"What does the doctor say?"

Dad exhales. "For a man my age, I'm doing great. Doctor says I could live another twenty years."

Twenty years. It's a long time. It isn't enough.

"One of the bypasses closed," he says quietly, almost so I can't hear him. "But they don't want to do anything about it. Not yet."

I feel my stomach descend down into my feet. "Did you tell Mom?"

He doesn't say anything, just shakes his head.

We both look at the surfboard, abandoned on the deck.

"I'll get it," I say. I pick it up and lean it against the far side wall.

"My strong, incredible daughter," he says. He pulls me toward him, and I feel his shallow sides, the way his body has thinned out. He used to be solid, more than a little round in the middle, but most of it is gone now.

I feel my chest constrict, and the water rise in my throat.

"Honey," he says. "Come on. Don't go there. Your old man is fine." He exhales out a long breath. "But you know no one lives forever."

"We're not at forever yet," I tell him. I lean my head on his shoulder.

"No, we're not!"

We watch the ocean like that for a moment.

"Surf sucked anyway," I say, and I feel his body relax against me—this tacit admission that I'm letting this one go.

He squeezes my shoulder.

"What do you say we make pancakes?" he says.

Dad heads inside to the kitchen, and I go upstairs. My hands shake as I unplug my phone and hit Leo's name. It rings once, twice, three times, and then I'm met with the familiar click of his voicemail. I throw it across the bed, and it lands, gingerly, on a pillow.

My fear transforms, morphs back into anger. Where is my husband?

The memory comes immediately, automatically. In one moment I'm in my childhood bedroom, and in the next I'm back in the worst moment of our marriage. Our final egg retrieval. The last time we did IVF.

Six months ago Leo and I showed up at the surgery center beaten down from the meds but excited. Relentless hope. It was still there. We had done our trigger shot thirty-six hours before, but the timing at the clinic was off and they rushed me into the surgery, afraid I'd ovulate before they could collect the eggs. All I saw was the OR fading to black and then coming to in the recovery room with Leo sitting beside me.

"How did it go?" I asked. "Did we get them?"

We had seen four eggs on our ultrasounds. We were hoping to capture all four. A dismal number for someone my age, but what amounted to a lot for us. We'd never had more than three.

"Dr. Park will be in soon," Leo said. He stood over me. He put a hand on my head, smoothed some hair down. I had lumbered into the waiting area with an ice pack pressed to my neck. I hadn't been able to drink anything for eight hours and had a headache from the lack of water. Now, I felt fine.

"What happened?" I asked him.

I saw it on his face—the way he was struggling to pull it together, to keep composed, to keep composed for me.

"Let's just wait," he told me.

As it turned out, we didn't get any.

"There was nothing of quality to retrieve," Dr. Park said. He was sympathetic, so were the nurses. Two of them came in to tell us better luck next time.

"Let's not lose hope," Dr. Park said. "There's a lot more we can do."

Leo stood up then. He walked to the corner of the room, where the curtain met the partition, and turned his back to us.

"Sorry," I whispered.

Dr. Park just nodded. "I'll let you get some rest."

He put a hand over mine, gently, and then took it away and was gone. I didn't blame him. I knew he had another patient going in, another set of eggs to retrieve. It wasn't his fault we hadn't gotten any. It wasn't anyone's. And if it were someone's, it was mine.

My eyes followed Leo. "Hello?"

I knew what was happening. I knew he was emotional. That he hadn't wanted Dr. Park to see his tears. But all I felt was rage.

Here I was, lying in a hospital bed, my insides having just been invaded, and there he was, sulking in a corner.

"Leo."

When he didn't move, I lost it.

"Could you please turn the fuck around?"

He did. I saw his eyes were red. "I can't do this anymore," he said.

I felt my insides boil. *He* couldn't do this anymore? He wasn't doing anything. I said as much.

"That is so not fair and you know it, Lauren. I don't want to spend our marriage this way. It's too painful. I think we maybe need to say enough is enough."

I felt breathless with his words.

"You just want to give up?" I felt enraged, tormented, even, that he didn't understand what that meant, that he wasn't looking at everything I had already given up, everything I had already sacrificed. That for him it was as easy as: *next*.

"I don't consider it giving up," he said. He was calm, rational. I wanted to kill him. "I consider it not prioritizing this fictional baby over ourselves."

"She's not fictional."

"Lauren," he said. I saw something soften in him. "How much pain do we have to go through?"

"There's no we here," I said. "You've done nothing. I'm the one in the hospital bed. I'm the one on all the hormones. I'm the one who can't exercise or drink for half the goddamn month. And you think this is your choice?"

It was nasty, mean-spirited. I was angry. I felt betrayed by him, abandoned. I felt what women throughout history have always felt—in service of someone else. That he could just decide not to have a baby, and I was powerless to get now what I so desperately wanted.

I thought about my ticket then. I thought about this opportunity I have. But I also knew it wouldn't work. Even this ticket couldn't fix it. What would I do? Go back to twenty-five? But I didn't want a baby. I wanted a baby with Leo.

We'd still do three more wishful-thinking IUIs after that, but when I think about our story, when things turned over, I think about that last retrieval.

The truth is nothing was ever the same afterward—and every month since, Leo has given up a little bit further. And I've resented him a little bit more.

I head downstairs to find the kitchen already a mess. Pans, bowls, blueberries popping on the stovetop, and butter melting on the griddle.

"How's Leo?" Dad asks. He looks at me sideways.

"No idea," I say.

Dad nods. "It's not easy being apart like this."

"I don't want to talk about it," I say.

I feel a bitterness spring up in me. Something that's been hidden now made front and center.

"Copy that." Dad goes to the freezer and pulls it open. "How do you feel about chocolate chips in the morning?"

"Decidedly pro."

We don't talk much more after that. We move around each other easily. Dad finishes up the batter; I make the blueberry syrup.

I add the chocolate chips in when the belly begins to bubble, and we eat at the breakfast table, just like we have so many times before.

I realize today is my third wedding anniversary.

CHAPTER NINETEEN

Stone calls the house and says it's not a good time for us to come over. Marcella and I don't go to see Bonnie. I work on the deck with coffee, then lunch, then a glass of wine as 3:00 p.m. turns into 4:00 p.m., and just before sunset, when I'm about to head inside, I see Stone at the bottom of the steps in the sand.

"I'm going out," he says. "You in?"

I pull on my suit, and at 7:25 we're catching our first wave.

The sun doesn't fully set until after nearly nine in the summer here, and the sky is hazy but bright. We're the only two people out on the water.

I watch Stone in the waves. The way his body slides through the ocean as if it's his partner. I shake my head because all at once I'm remembering what that feels like—to move against him.

"You're even better than you used to be," I say.

He turns around to look at me. I see the rise and fall of his chest against his board. "I think I'm better when I'm with you."

"That's not true." I think about Board Up. All the time he's spent practicing, devoted to this sport in my absence. And all the time I've spent away from the water. "But I feel it, too."

I see the goose bumps on his skin like a road map. I trail my eyes down his arms and follow his fingers into the ocean.

He looks up at me. Blinks some water away.

"What do you feel?"

"Connected," I say, without pause. "And humbled."

"Always humbled," Stone says. "I forget when I haven't been in the real deal long enough."

"That you can't take it for granted?"

Stone looks at me. I see the glass droplets on his eyelashes. "That she's ruthless."

I think about this. How many missed opportunities there have been on the ocean. How many waves I've blundered, skipped, straight-up ignored. How many I've fought and lost. How many have held me under, forced me to fight to breathe.

"Yeah but the waves keep coming, right?"

The sky starts to change around us. I feel a stab of fear that even this thing I know so well—have known so intimately—could destroy me in a second.

"Death and taxes and waves," Stone says. He reaches across the water. Gives my shoulder a squeeze.

We sit that way, looking at each other, as the sunset changes from orange to pink to blue.

"We should head in," Stone says.

I follow his lead. We paddle into the next set and ride it straight to the shore. I fall in on the end and come up sputtering to see Stone dragging his board out of the water.

He drops his and comes back to help me, but I knock him off. "I got it," I say. "You want dinner?"

I've avoided talking about Bonnie, our canceled plans, what it means.

"I do," he says. "But I should head back. I've just been picking up for me and Dad lately."

"I'll tell Sylvia to make extra."

Stone waves me off. "We're fine, really."

"She'd love to," I say. "It's the least we can do."

He hooks his board under his arm. He pauses. The night is violet around us, now. Almost iridescent. "I'm glad you're here, Laur," he says, and then he's gone.

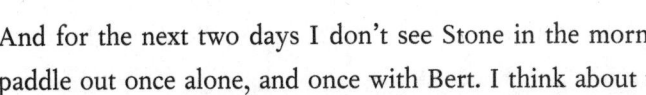

And for the next two days I don't see Stone in the mornings. I paddle out once alone, and once with Bert. I think about texting him, but in our month back at the beach neither of us has reignited our thread. I've pulled it up. The last exchange is from six years ago. An unanswered one from me: *How are you?*

Marcella calls Jeff and drops food off with them. It makes us all feel better to know, at least, that they're eating.

I still haven't heard more than a text here and there from Leo. Most of them begin or end with *sorry*. I know he's busy, and when I feel my resentment turn to apathy, it doesn't really bother me.

Tonight Sylvia is working on some mixed-media art project and retires to the back house after dinner, Styrofoam and tin foil in hand. I see Pea trail after her, unwanted, but Sylvia lets her in the door.

"I'll finish up the kitchen," I tell my parents, and they head up the stairs, yawning, waving thanks.

Tonight's dinner was a fava bean stew with roast chicken, and the pans are gritty, oiled, and plentiful. This is going to take a while.

I pour some soap, turn up the water to scalding, and open Spotify.

We always listened to Bob Marley in the house growing up, and every time I'm out here I still crave it—that easy, soulful, beach music.

I put on a mix and get to work scrubbing. I'm about halfway through "Waiting in Vain" when I hear a knock at the back door.

I look up to see Stone standing there.

I move to open it, but before I can even let the latch up I see it in his face—she's gone.

"Stone," I say.

He nods once, slowly, and then he moves toward me. Stumbles, really, and instinctively I reach out and catch him. I hold him steady as he folds into my shoulder. Long, shallow sobs that move both our bodies but have almost no sound.

"Come on," I say. "Come in."

He pulls back. He shakes his head. "I need to go," he says. "I need to get out of here."

I pull back. I look at him. I don't know if he's saying he needs to leave Malibu or if he's asking something else, asking something of me.

"OK," I say. "I'll drive."

CHAPTER TWENTY

I take us to the parking lot at the Trancas Country Mart. Or my hands take us. One minute we are on the PCH, and the next we are turning off at the Starbucks. I see a young woman behind the counter taking the order of an elderly couple.

The place is entirely different than it was when we were growing up here. There were no trendy boutiques or brunch places. It was the rodeo. A solid sandwich shop, a hardware store, and a coffee spot that had one kind of milk.

The center is nearly closed. The waiters are hovering over their last, lingering customers, and all the storefronts are shuttered.

I park, kill the engine, and roll down the windows.

"Do you want coffee?" I ask. Sometimes Starbucks stays open until ten. It's 9:53.

Stone shakes his head. "No," he says. "Thanks."

"We could drive down to the water."

"This is good," he says. "This is perfect."

We sit in silence like this, letting the moments pile up. Stone is one of the few people I can be completely quiet with, because silence is part of our language. There was so much that happened between us that had nothing to do with words.

There was a decade spent on the water, feeling the ocean, communicating for hours with just our bodies. We could read each other back then. We knew when one person was hungry or tired or frustrated or horny. We didn't have to say it. I wonder if we're now, after this past month, speaking to each other in this way again.

"It was really bad," he says, after many minutes have passed. "The end was gruesome. Peaceful death, all that shit—" He punches his fist against the glove compartment. "She didn't deserve that."

"No," I say.

"I should have done it differently."

I turn to look at him. He looks to me like he did when we were kids. Young, innocent, a golden surfer boy.

"You were there," I say.

Stone shakes his head. He's never been a crier. I think I saw him cry only once in the twenty-five years I've known him, not even the day we broke up. But the tears come fast now.

"I couldn't help her. I couldn't make it less painful." He wipes the back of his hand against his cheeks. "I should have insisted she have morphine. I should have made that decision for her, fuck what she wanted. Her doctor, that quack . . ." He wipes the back of his hand across his face. "I wasn't even there when it happened. I went out to get a fucking bagel."

His voice trails off, and I feel a hot sting in my chest. I feel like a monster.

I could fix this for him. I could give him the ability to go back and make it better. He could give her morphine; he could say goodbye. Her death will haunt him for the rest of his life, and I won't do a thing about it.

I've felt the guilt before, of course I have. The world is full of tragedy. There are fires that kill thousands of people, guns that kill hundreds at a clip. I could stop it, maybe. Travel there, capture the ember, point out the backpack. I could help. Every day, every year, there are things I could undo, deaths I could prevent, families torn apart I could mend.

Stone hangs his head. His shoulders shake. I feel helpless. No, more than that—I feel ashamed. I feel this power like an albatross. I feel its weight.

I want to make this better for him. My heart cinches at the revelation: I want to fix it.

I reach out and grab his hand. He curls his fingers around mine and then brings them to his chest. I can feel his heart—steady, rapid beats.

"Lauren," he says. Just that, just my name.

And then, as if in slow motion, he bring his mouth down to kiss our interlaced palms. I feel the cool weight of his skin on me, the wet press of his lips.

"Yes," I answer, but it's not a question, not really.

I can hear my blood in my ears as if it's an impending tsunami. *Run run run. Get to higher ground.*

"I'm sorry," he says, but his lips don't leave my hand. Instead, they trail over my fingers, stopping to open my palm and explore the pad of my thumb.

It feels like a train is about to leave, is leaving, has already left. His mouth finds the curve of my wrist.

His hands are on my arm now. Exploring the belly of my bicep.

I want him to name it. I want him to tell me, right here in this car, what it is that is happening. We were so young when we were together that we rarely expressed ourselves at all. I have so few memories of him telling me anything. Of any truth that wasn't just our bodies.

"I can't believe you're here right now," he says, as if I've spoken it aloud. "I can't believe it's you."

I exhale a shaky breath. He stops what he's doing and looks at me. Our eyes lock, and in that moment I see only us, only what was once uncomplicated by life. Before money and fertility and practicality mattered. When life was all possibility.

"I still think about it," he says, and when he does it feels like a door opening, like a breeze blowing in. "I want to say I miss you, but it's not strong enough."

I close my eyes against his words, but it doesn't matter, they are already inside. I feel them down deep, into my stomach. They buzz and course through me like swallowed honeybees.

When I open my eyes, Stone is still looking at me.

"Nothing has turned out how I thought it would. I never should have left. I never should have fucked up what we had."

"Why did you?" I have been waiting more than a decade to ask this question, to get the answer.

He exhales out. He seems, all at once, frustrated.

"Because I thought I didn't know enough yet to choose. I was young. I didn't know you don't get to decide, life decides for you."

"I chose," I say.

Stone nods, but it's not just an admission, it's movement. It's toward me. His fingers move over mine. His thumb caresses the back of my wrist.

He looks up at me, and in his eyes I see all of it—all the pain of the loss, of this moment, of everything he cannot undo. I see Bonnie and his family and dinners around her table. I see the years spread out like a map—all the weaving ways life has taken us from each other and wound us back together, back to this moment.

This moment that is both an extension and a collapsing.

And so I do the only thing I can, the only thing I know how to do right here and now in this car: I take us out of it.

I reach over and thread my fingers through his hair. I know, because I know everything—that he doesn't always shower after the ocean, that his hair will grow crusty with salt water. I feel the birthmark, raised, on the back of his neck, trail my fingers down the constellation of freckles below his right ear.

It's like a house, I think. One I could sleepwalk through and never hit a wall.

I thread my thumb over his lips, and then his arms are cupping my back and we are kissing.

His lips land on mine, hard, and he pulls me toward him—toward the passenger seat. He unclicks my seat belt, never letting his hands leave my body, and then I'm climbing over the center console and straddling his lap.

My legs hit the seat belt buckle and my backside is crammed up against the glove compartment.

"God," Stone says. "I missed you."

I lean down my head in answer. His mouth is open and hot. I remember those small, urgent kisses from when we were teens. When we had ten minutes, maybe even less, to make each other's bodies rise and fall in quiet corners of the house.

It's hot in here. The windows start to steam.

I pull off my shirt.

I let him trail his fingers down my stomach, over my shoulders and breasts. One hand travels down, down, until it presses against me—*yes, there*—and the other cups the back of my head. His mouth is on my neck, behind my ear.

I feel this moment like a kaleidoscope—all the memories blending and merging together. Us on our boards, on towels in the sand, in my bedroom right before dawn. In this parking lot, fifteen years ago.

Stone pulls his lips from mine and kisses my neck, the dip of my collarbone. "I remember you," he whispers into my body. So does she.

The rest of our clothes, gone. I feel his body naked against mine. The most new and familiar thing.

Sex with Stone felt like being let into a vault. It was like he had the key and was unlocking this secret, valuable world. And I was terrified—for years after—that our experience together wasn't our experience at all but his. That it was his presence and talent and touch that made it special, and that he could replicate it with anyone else he wanted. That all the sex he had was that connected and precious. For years after, I couldn't think about it without crying—what his body was gifting someone else. What he was sharing—readily, frequently—that I could never seem to replicate.

But here, now, I know it wasn't him, but *us*. Some seismic, hormonal grafting that makes our bodies designed for each other. That makes this moment feel like all the ones before it. Like we've only ever been here.

It feels like we are traveling back, closing the space between what we were and are. Time is an accordion—it expands and then collapses, expands and collapses.

I move my hips against his, slowly and then more urgently.

"Come for me," he says, and I let myself go in the way I haven't for so long. I let myself go like I'm sixteen again, in this very same parking lot, with this very same man.

CHAPTER TWENTY-ONE

We sit in silence for a few minutes afterward—breathing against each other.

Stone hands me my shirt. I put it on. We get dressed slowly and then quickly, covering what we were just moments ago so desperate to reveal. Stone has ended up in the driver's seat and me in the passenger.

He kisses the side of my head and then, without asking, puts my car in reverse and drives us home.

We pull up to the house, but neither of us makes a move to get out.

"I want to say something," he says. "But I don't know exactly what, and I'm afraid of getting it wrong."

I also have no idea. Because to say something and have it matter means the undoing of so much. And yet to have it not matter, to have it be anecdotal, is somehow just as bad.

"I don't think we should," I say. "Right? Maybe we shouldn't say anything."

So much of the tension that filled up this car has dissolved now. What is left in its place, tomorrow, will be grief for Bonnie.

"OK," he says. "We won't."

"Are you going to be able to sleep?" I ask him.

"Better odds now." He picks up my hand, interlaces our fingers. I feel the pull of something again, the thing that connects us, tugging. "I'll see you tomorrow?"

I nod. He will, of course he will. I live here now.

He hovers there, right next to me. I think that maybe he's going to kiss me, but he just squeezes my hand once, twice, and gets out to open my door.

We walk up the steps in silence.

"Bonnie loved you so much," I say. "You were hers in every sense of the word."

He nods. A tear escapes down his cheek. "Fuck," he says.

I press my face to his, hold my cheek against his cheek, and then he opens the door, and all at once I'm inside, and Stone isn't.

I take a deep breath. I put my hands on my abdomen and exhale. But they come, anyway. The sharp pains. They arrive with such intensity that it's everything I can do not to scream and wake the house.

I feel the night like a knife. It cuts through me.

Bonnie is gone, and I have betrayed Leo.

What have I done?

I think about Stone's hands on my stomach, the naked curve of his shoulders, so familiar to me, even after all this time. I shut my eyes and shake my head to clear the images.

I pull my phone out of my bag. I have a missed call from Leo. I click on the voicemail.

Hey, babe, just finishing up, I know it's late. Shooting starts tomorrow. I'm sorry I've been so MIA . . .

There's a pause in his message. I hold my breath.

I miss you, baby.

I click the phone off before the message ends. I can't catch my breath. I feel like I'm going to have a heart attack right here in the living room.

I can't do this. I can't bear it. I'm not this woman. I cannot have had an affair. I cannot have cheated. This cannot be my reality.

I race up the stairs. I feel the blood in my fingers, throbbing pinpricks, like insects are stinging every surface of my skin.

Oh God oh God oh God.

Leo. My husband. Who has gone with me to fertility appointments and held my hair back when I've been sick from supermarket sushi. Who has made the bed haphazardly in the morning because he knows it's important to me and puts my shoes away when I leave them by the door. We have memories, too. We have a kaleidoscope of them. But they are mundane memories, everyday memories. It's not just the last IVF or the engagement or the wedding. It's all the moments in between. The ones that are hard to remember because they fade into the fabric of a marriage.

What is it about distance that lends itself so easily to fantasy? What is it about familiarity that doesn't?

I don't make the decision to do it, the moment chooses for me. Our rabbi, every Yom Kippur, would talk about readiness. How we are never ready for life's big moments—the moments that choose us, is how she'd put it—but that we must trust God in those moments to show up. That we are not alone.

But I don't need God. At least, not tonight. I have something better.

One moment I'm wringing my hands at the top of the stairs, and the next I'm crouched next to the safe in the guest room—the one that has been an office and a painting studio and is now filled with various odds and ends—a dust-covered Peloton bike, boxes of itemized photos, old outdoor couch cushions, suitcases.

It swings open, same code.

Inside are our birth certificates, some jewelry—a string of pearls my mother gifted me that I never wear, small diamond hoops, a jade amulet—and, of course, my ticket.

I take it out. I hold it in my hands. It's not smaller or lighter or heavier than I remember. It's exactly as I've always pictured it to be. I try to think about the last time I looked at it. Years ago, maybe even a decade. I was always too afraid to touch it, too afraid that my brain might betray me and I'd find myself somewhere I didn't need to be, having squandered it.

This, I think.

It's small, the kind of ticket you rip off by the roll at a county fair—and for a moment my stomach sinks. It's not real, it's not true. It's all just been a story, a fable. It was a fairy tale my mother made up, that she was told, too. It's the tale of our lineage, nothing more. It won't work.

And it's this disbelief that pushes me over, truthfully. Because I need to know, now. I need to know if it's all just been make believe. I need to know if anything about our story—hers and hers and hers and mine—is real.

And so I use it. I wind us to a time before. The betrayal, the car, the Greek, dinner, Paradise Cove, the beach. I turn it all back.

And it feels euphoric to spend it, to open the coffer and blow it all out. To finally let go of the thing I am most closely holding.

What happened is gone, and so is my ticket.

CHAPTER TWENTY-TWO

I wake up to an alarm. But it's not an alarm, it's Leo calling. I blink up in bed and swat my nightstand until I unhook my phone.

"Hi," I say, near croak.

"Hey." I hear the sounds of the city behind him—awake and talking. "You and Pea leaving for the beach soon? I thought I could catch you."

I open my eyes. I'm in our house, in West Hollywood. It's Friday. I'm supposed to drive out to the beach tonight. To start this summer.

I scramble up in bed. "Leo?"

"Yeah? Can you hear me? Babe? Sorry, there's a siren."

I press my eyes closed. *Oh my God, it worked.*

"Hi, no, I'm here, I can hear you."

"How's it going? You driving out to the beach tonight?"

I look at my packed suitcases, think about the renter who is supposed to come tomorrow. Pea's crate. Change of plans.

"I'm not going to the beach," I say. I find out what is happening as I say it. "I'm coming to New York to be with you."

I hear Leo's laugh on the other end. "Laur, babe, you're scaring me."

"No!" I say. "I mean, I'm so proud of you. I want to see you in action. And I don't want to spend the summer at the beach. I want to be with you. I'm booking a ticket now."

The siren passes. "Lauren? Are you sure? I'm working a ton, the hours are kind of intense. I'm not sure how much . . ."

"I'm coming, Leo."

A cacophony of cars honk. "I love it," he says. "I guess text me when you're landing? I could try to grab an Uber out to meet you. And see if Tanya will take Pea."

Our neighbor has two cats that Pea vaguely hates but who won't put up much of a fuss if she wants to rule the roost for the summer.

"I have it under control," I say. "Just tell me where we're going home to. I'll meet you there."

"Home!" he says. "It's a walk-up in Brooklyn, but, baby, if you're there, it will be."

The rest is easy. Things are easy when you are running.

I book a flight, pack my bags, and send my mom a text: *Going to be with Leo in New York for a bit. Call you from there.*

Tanya comes to pick up Pea. She barely manages a meow as I hand her off.

"I'll miss you," I say.

Tanya snuggles her close. "We're going to spend the summer gardening. I hope you like tomatoes!"

I get to the airport an hour early, there's hardly a line at security, and then I'm seated in 18J.

The flight feels like it goes on forever. I just want to see him. Wrap my arms around him. I know when I get to him I'll feel grounded, reoriented. I know when I get to him I'll forget. It'll be like it never happened, because it didn't.

We land into a rainstorm. There are some delays on the ground, trying to find a gate, but once we are guided in we deboard quickly. I take the escalator down to baggage claim, and there, at the bottom of the steps, is Leo.

He's holding a sign: *My Wife*, and as soon as I see it, and him, I take off running. I push past people, my rolling bag nipping at my ankles, and then I'm in his arms. He catches me, his body holds the force.

"Hi," he says into my ear. "I had to give you a proper welcome."

"I love you," I say. I take in his smell, his warmth, the strength of his body. How did I forget? "I love you, I love you, I love you."

"I love you, too."

It's not until we pull apart that I realize I am crying.

"What?" Leo asks. "What's wrong?"

I shake my head. "Nothing," I say. "I'm just happy."

"Be happy with less tears," he says. "We're OK, right?"

I look into his eyes.

"Right."

CHAPTER TWENTY-THREE

Leo lifts my bag off the carousel, and we wind our way out of arrivals and through the parking structure.

"One of the guys lent me their car," Leo says.

He heaves my duffel into the back of a Kia Sorento and then comes around and opens my door for me. "M'lady."

Inside smells like peanuts and pine cone air freshener. I feel simultaneously nostalgic and nauseous.

Leo gets inside. He always waits until the car starts beeping at him to put on his seat belt, and it drives me crazy. I start to say something and then stop myself.

"How did your parents take it?" he asks.

"I texted my mom."

Leo looks at me. "Jesus, Lauren. You have to be nicer to her."

"No, I know. I'll call her when we get there."

Leo takes my hand. "She deserves a little more than you give her, sometimes."

I push out a breath. "Sometimes."

We head to Brooklyn. Production rented Leo a second-story apartment in Cobble Hill that's full of light and crown molding.

It's simple—the kitchen is half bathroom—but I love it. I'd love anything.

The walls are painted cheerful colors—dusty rose for the bedroom, yellow for the living/dining area. And the kitchen cabinets are robin's-egg blue.

"This place is great," I tell him. "I love it." I flip down onto the pastel velvet love seat. "I could live here."

Leo laughs. "I don't think we can afford to live here."

I study him from the couch. He's lost a few pounds these past few weeks; he always does when he's working. Too focused, too busy. He hasn't shaved in at least a week—stubble filling in, turning to an almost beard. I like it.

I put my bags in the foyer. It's hot in New York—it's July, after all—but inside the apartment it's the perfect breezy temperature. The windows are open—no screens—and briefly I wonder if we have to worry about mosquitoes the way we do in West Hollywood, but Leo pulls me out of it.

"Come here," he says. He pulls me down into an armchair with him.

I put my arms around his neck. He leans down and kisses me.

"Hi," he says.

I look up at him. "Hi," I say. I take a deep breath. "Listen, I've been thinking."

"Uh-oh," Leo says. "Already?"

"You were right."

"About what?"

"The fertility stuff."

Immediately, I feel him stiffen. The word is unwanted.

"I know you wanted to give up."

He doesn't say anything, doesn't fight me on it.

"It's just—there's been this horrible unspoken thing between us for months now, maybe longer, and I want it to be over. I want to give up, too."

Leo's face doesn't change. I press my fingers into his tight trap muscles, kneading them there.

"I'm done," I say.

His brow furrows, he shakes his head. "I thought—"

"Listen, Leo. This life we have, I've been missing it." My voice breaks because I realize how true it is, how everything I'm saying is the absolute, definitive truth I've just been too spun out to see it. "I want it back."

I remember, in all my single years, being afraid of what marriage might demand of me—the time I'd have to give another person, what a huge commitment it would be, if I ever even got there. And then I met Leo. I remember a night, almost six months into dating, when we were talking about our future. Even in those early days, when we were trying to fit our worlds together, there was so little conflict. It wasn't so much that I thought he was *the one* but that I couldn't see a natural end. With everyone else, there had been an obvious future off-ramp. With Leo, there was nothing but open road. And I knew, even then, that we were going to make it stick.

I remember asking him what he wanted to do for his birthday the following month—a big one, forty—and becoming seized by the age. Not because we felt real or adult, although we were and are all those things—but because I all at once realized all the time that had passed in his life without me, all the years where he blew out candles and I wasn't by his side.

I believed, in a strange way, when I was single, that when I met my person the clock would reset. That I, too, would be twenty-seven again, like all my friends had been. That I'd get it all back. That decade of singlehood, of searching. That our young marriage would be just that: young. But that's not what happened, of course, and now, being here with Leo, I realize how long I spent wishing for everything we have. And how much I don't want to waste what comes next—what's already here.

"This life we have," I tell him again. "It's the only one I want. And I don't want us to miss it because we're so busy trying to get to a different one."

Leo's eyes fill. In another moment, a tear falls down his cheek. I wipe it away.

"You're right," I say. "And I'm sorry for us. I know how much you want to be a dad. I want it, too—But it's enough."

Leo shakes his head. His hands find my waist. He holds me firmly. "Do you really mean that?"

I feel my chest exhale. Everything I've been holding, released. "Yes, I mean it. I love you. Let's give up."

Leo laughs. He touches his nose down to meet mine. "Let's give up."

He kisses me then—deep and rooted. I fold my body into his. I think about the idea of home, of what it is. It was the beach for so long and then it was the idea of our family, this imagined future, our baby. But right now I think that maybe home could be us. It could be this apartment in Brooklyn. It could be now. Home could be this very moment, if we make it.

CHAPTER TWENTY-FOUR

The days and weeks after the accident are euphoric—Marcella has done it, she has successfully taken it back—but once the shock wears off she is left with a low-simmer depression that turns, in a matter of hours, into a boil. One morning she is clipping roses looking at her husband reading, and by the afternoon she is crouched in the corner of her bathroom clutching her stomach in the midst of what can only be described as a panic attack.

Because she understands, now. The flip side. The thing, perhaps, her mother was trying to protect her from. Life offered the worst to her, and she could undo it. What will happen now that she cannot?

She goes to Sylvia. She asks how she can live like this, what happened after her mother spent hers.

"I never put much stock in it," Sylvia tells her. "I used it on something relatively innocuous. I never had anything that worthy of taking back."

When Sylvia says it, it feels like a slight to Marcella, like the tragedy in Marcella's life is by intention, not accident. Like she has done something to make it so.

"But what about my dad?" Marcella asks.

"Why would I have used it to bring back a man who didn't want to be here?"

Her mother has never used the words that succinctly, has never said it that way, without filler.

"Why didn't he want to?" Marcella asks.

Sylvia shrugs. They are outside on the deck. Below them the ocean presents and bows, presents and bows. It should be relaxing, it always was, but now it reminds Marcella of the cyclical nature of time. The way things repeat, circle back.

Sylvia puts a hand on Marcella's knee. She leans forward, into her. "I don't know," she says. "I never got the chance to ask. When we met we were both young, and family wasn't something either of us spoke about. It just happened. I knew I could take care of you alone. Even before you were born, I was certain of it."

Marcella holds a tight smile. She is not certain, though. Her mother left her for long stretches of time in the company of neighbors. She learned how to cook at seven years old out of necessity. All she ever wanted was the stability of family, what she has now, and the fact that it could be taken away—that it was—leaves her breathless.

Help me, she wants to say. *Help me live like this.* But if her mother can't help her, then at least she can help her daughter. Lauren. She needs to know.

"We're going to tell her," Marcella says to Sylvia.

Sylvia looks to her. Few things make Sylvia scared, but Marcella can tell that this is one.

"No," Sylvia says. "It's not right."

"She's my daughter," Marcella says.

Sylvia tries to fight her on it, but what does she know? She might have made the best decision she could in waiting to tell her, but it was the wrong one. Marcella will not make the same mistake with Lauren. Lauren will live her life with full awareness. She will know what she has, how precious it is. She will make the choice on when to use it, and if they show her, if they express the significance, she will choose wisely. Tragedy will never find her unarmed.

Marcella does not understand her daughter, no, but she loves her. She will do anything to make her life easier. She regrets to admit this, but she wants her daughter to live with more ease. She wants her to live more closely to Sylvia.

Lauren finds her first. In the shower, the following day, crouched on the floor, the cascade of water running over her.

Lauren turns off the showerhead. "What is wrong with you?" she wants to know.

They sit her down in her room. For a moment Marcella thinks about how small Lauren looks on the bed, and how young the decor in this room is. They should get her something new, something besides this paisley bedspread and pink floral curtains. She is not girly, she never has been, and Marcella wonders why she did not notice before, why she ever picked this out at all.

"We have something other people don't," Sylvia says.

"What kind of thing?" Lauren asks, already, impossibly, getting it.

Later, after her questions and their council, Marcella feels lighter. Like in having the conversation she has relived herself of something significant.

It does not occur to her that the burden has not been extinguished but shared. That along with the gift, she has placed the weight onto her daughter's shoulders as well.

CHAPTER TWENTY-FIVE

Life in New York is idyllic. Nora Ephron great. For days, weeks, we have nothing but sunshine, cold sauvignon blanc, fifteen thousand daily steps, sex and harmony. I almost can't believe how happy we are, how happy I am. From the moment I land we are just where we were always trying to get to. I don't even remember feeling this way in the beginning of our relationship. Meeting Leo felt not like a puzzle piece snapping down into place but a softening. The point was not that our corners fit but that he dissolved mine. But now—now I can feel myself sharpening. In using my ticket I have done a lot more than choose to go back. I've chosen. And in some ways it feels like for the very first time. I feel powerful, omniscient. I turned the whole world back. I did it. I can do anything.

And it's this knowledge of power that makes the decision to stop trying for a baby not so much a sacrifice but a shedding. Of the woman who wanted that—the one who was so clearly clinging to a sinking ship. All I had to do was let go and float to the surface.

"We miss you here," Dad says on the phone two weeks later. His voice is quiet, but he's outside, and the waves wash out every other word.

"I miss you, too," I say. "But New York is amazing. I'm really so glad I came."

Today is Tuesday, and Leo had an early-morning shoot, which means he'll be wrapped by six, and I'm headed to meet him for a celebratory dinner at Gramercy Tavern. We never go to fancy meals—we can't afford it, and in Los Angeles, it doesn't seem worth it—but now we are people with $5,000 of disposable income and no upcoming fertility bills. We decided to celebrate our anniversary in style.

"I'm glad you two are happy," he says.

"How are you?" I say. I am distracted. I am trying to pick out a dress to wear. It is too hot for jeans, and everything summery I own makes me look like I'm in an L.L.Bean catalog. I settle on some black crepe shorts and a white T-shirt and heels. Sophisticated, not trying too hard.

"Did Mom tell you?" Dad says.

"What?"

I peer close into the mirror, applying lipstick.

"Stone is back."

I hold the coral shade to my lips. Of course he is back. Just because I'm not there, doesn't mean he isn't.

"She didn't mention it."

"He came because Bonnie wasn't doing so well. You know she's been sick for a while, right? But she seems to be responding to this new trial they have her in."

New trial. This makes me stop.

"What new trial?"

"I don't know. Something Stone campaigned for. I guess he came out here and ended up convincing her to do it, and it worked. Good news."

Good news. All at once, I feel breathless. I close my eyes and open them again. Is it possible that this wasn't just a reset for me but for him? For all of us? Bonnie—alive and improving.

I haven't let myself think about that night. Sometimes, when Leo falls asleep (immediately, always) and I'm lying in bed, my mind will wander right up to the seam of it. But I don't cross the line. There's nowhere to put it. There's nowhere to put it because it never actually happened.

But now I see that not only did it not happen but things *had* to happen this way. It was only in taking it back that we got what we were really meant for. And now it's not just true for me and Leo—it's true for Stone and Bonnie, too.

"That's incredible," I say.

Stone is not with me—in the ocean, at breakfast—at the edge of the Greek. And with that time he's changed Bonnie's mind. With that time he's saved her life. There's been nothing for him to do but be close to her, exactly as he wanted.

"Yes," Dad says. "Let's hope it stays that way, but it's looking really promising."

"It will," I say, firmer than I mean it. "I know it."

"Where are you guys off to tonight?" Dad asks, changing the subject.

"Gramercy Tavern," I say. I cap the lipstick, pick up my bronzer brush.

Dad whistles. "Fancy."

"We're celebrating," I say, more defensive than I mean to be.

Dad pauses. "It's a good thing," he says.

"Yeah," I say. "I know."

He wants to talk more then. About New York and the weather and if I think Brooklyn is better than Manhattan these days, the way everyone says. But I'm rushing to get off the phone. I have to send half an hour's worth of emails, and I should be on the subway in fifteen minutes.

"All right," he says. "I get the hint."

"I'll call you next week!"

We hang up, and I pull my shirt over my head—careful to avoid the makeup—open my laptop, and settle on the couch.

The place in Brooklyn is happy, and I've found myself falling into a rhythm here. I wake up and go for a walk, stop for a coffee at one of the plethora of hipster bean shops. I've taken to having a cortado, which I didn't even know existed before I got here but now I don't think I can possibly live without. Then I come back to the Henry Street apartment and work from the couch. Leo leaves early—usually before I'm up—and I have the place to myself.

I'm normally able to finish my work before Los Angeles is even conscious, which leaves the second part of the day for exploring. I'll take the F train into the city and begin there, or I'll explore Brooklyn. I venture out to Red Hook, visit art galleries and restaurants that only serve oysters and champagne on tap. I fondle trinkets in the real-life Etsy storefronts—candles shaped like elephants, hand-blown glass napkin rings.

When I hit a lull, or the ninety-degree summer heat becomes too much to bear, I'll pop into a coffee shop and order an iced cortado with cinnamon and sit in the air-conditioning while I eat a chocolate chip cookie the size of my hand.

I pull on a white eyelet shirt and tuck it into the crepe shorts I already have on. I find a pair of black strappy sandals—no heel—grab a black faux leather clutch I bought at the farmers market in Brentwood, and head out the door.

The New York night is weighted. In Los Angeles even a one-hundred-degree day burns off into the seventies by 8:00 p.m., but in New York the heat lingers, sits like a first date closing down a bar.

I hop on the F, which everyone is telling me is nightmarish but actually seems totally fine. The train is about 70 percent empty, and in thirty minutes I'm being spit out onto Sixth Avenue at Fourteenth Street.

I'll be about ten minutes early to dinner, so I take my time walking over to Fifth and then up to Twentieth Street. Flatiron is buzzing with activity—it's a summer night in the city, and people are out enjoying the weather. A crew of Rollerbladers rolls down as a group of teenagers dips into an apartment building on lower Fifth. Seventeenth Street between Fifth and Sixth seems to be shut down for an evening fair, and adults enjoy open-air wine as kids run up and down the block chasing giant bubbles and balloon animals.

Everyone is always talking about how New York isn't what it used to be, how the city is empty, how apartments sit vacant, and yet—the streets are packed, property values are on the rise. Nothing stays static forever, I think. But why is the past always memorialized as better? I never spent time in New York when I was young, but now that I'm less young I'm here and enjoying every beat of what *this* New York is delivering.

Leo is already at the restaurant when I arrive, hovering by the door.

"You're here," I say. Ten minutes late for Leo is on time. I'm used to it.

"I am," he says. "I had to run uptown and drop some stuff with post. Didn't take as long as I expected."

He cocks his head to the side, taking me in. "You look great."

"So do you."

He's wearing khakis and a short-sleeved button-down. He has some TOMS slides on. He looks casual, relaxed, even if his forehead is beading up with sweat.

I give him a quick kiss. "Hi."

"Hey, babe. Let's go in before I melt."

He opens the door, and I duck under his arm. He glides a hand onto my waist as I pass by him. I smell his cologne—something he hasn't worn in so long. Cardamom and red wine. He smells like winter here tastes, and I imagine us walking into the same restaurant in December, snow on the ground.

The inside of Gramercy Tavern is old and oaken. We are having dinner in the Dining Room, which feels like a cross between a New York institution and a cozy den. As soon as we walk in, I immediately feel underdressed.

Men in suits with jackets slung over their chairs and sleeves pushed up to their elbows sit across from women in slim-fit black pants engrossed in their iPhones. The walls are cream, and there are high, dark beams overhead, heavy curtains separating the Dining Room from the bar and soft overhead lighting. If New York is not what it used to be, then this is what it was.

Leo raises his eyebrows at me. *Fancy.*

I wiggle them back. *Do we dare?*

Our last anniversary we spent in the hallway between our bedroom and bathroom. We had had plans to go out—pasta at our favorite, Donna's, in Echo Park. We loved the cozy bar, simple sauce, and the fact that the owner, Michael, Negroni in hand, seemed to inhabit the place like a home, not a restaurant.

But my period came, the day before, and I was wrecked with pain. For some, fertility treatment has a negligent impact on their cycle, but for me it was brutal. I felt doubled over in cramps, nausea, breast tenderness that made my B cup start sleeping in a bra. Every time I took it off and let them down, it felt like I'd been punched in the chest.

I roll my shoulders, dislodging the memory. Tonight is not about one line or Clomid for a full fourteen days. Tonight is about *us*. Life is about us now.

We are seated at a table that is far too big for the two of us—square mahogany, set to perfection. We square off a corner of it as the waiter pulls back my chair.

"Someone will be over momentarily. I hear we are celebrating. Would either of you care for a glass of champagne?"

"Please," Leo says, gesturing to me.

I open and close my mouth in a way I hope communicates *Same*.

"We can't afford this," I tell Leo. "Can we?"

"Baby, I have a thousand dollars in twenties in my pocket."

Leo's pay is good, but the best part of the gig is that he gets a per diem. Every day, one hundred dollars in cash. Leo stuffs all of it into a Ziplock bag and hands me a wad every couple of days. I feel flush with cash.

When was the last time someone paid in cash here? Could we pass for the mob? I look at Leo. Probably not with the TOMS.

"Besides," Leo says. "Tonight isn't about *can't*. We're here. We're happy."

"We're more than that," I say. I lean over and reach for him, thread my arms around his neck and kiss his mouth.

Our champagne arrives. Leo lifts his glass. "To the next chapter," he says. He gets serious. He puts his hand on top of mine. "I don't think I can remember ever loving you more. Thank you."

For our first wedding anniversary Leo and I went to Maui. We rented a little place in a town called Paia—an Airbnb that had no

AC and a half-functional mosquito net—but we loved it. We'd walk Baldwin Beach in the morning and go to the Fish Market for tacos and tuna burgers at night.

We rented a car, and one day we drove over to Wailea—a more touristy area, where the big, fancy hotels are. Everyone said we had to go to the Four Seasons for drinks, so we did. We sat in their sprawling, airy lobby with picture-perfect ocean views and a stream of light Hawaiian music. We ordered twenty-seven-dollar cocktails and eighteen-dollar edamame and picked at it until sundown.

Leo wore khaki shorts and a loud Hawaiian-print shirt. Something purple and orange we had picked up at ABC Stores, mostly as a joke. I remember looking at my hulking, sweating, out-of-place husband—who was only in that hotel and on that island to make me happy—and thinking that if there were ever anything I could do to put his happiness first, I'd do it.

Leo runs his thumb over the back of my hand. I feel bathed in his warmth, the warmth of us, of our marriage, and I think how happiness is determined not by getting what you want but by determining which things to hold on to and which things to let go. That there is joy in relinquishing. How extraordinary it is to be given the second chance to see the path we were always meant to travel down.

In the early days of our marriage, I'd look at Leo and feel terrified of how much I loved him. Because to love him meant to be decimated at losing him. To love him that deeply meant that my happiness was now in someone else's hands. And it wasn't just the love, it was the reliance. As time went on we became like an ecosystem. We needed each other for sunlight and shelter and food and water. We needed each other to grow.

But sitting with Leo now I don't feel the weight of us, of everything that might come our way—of even our dependence. I feel the ease of the now, the way the universe seems to be rewarding our pivot with nothing but open road. A true new beginning.

"Thank you," I say. *Thank you, thank you, thank you.*

CHAPTER TWENTY-SIX

The call doesn't come super late at night or super early in the morning, either. It does not wake me out of sleep. Instead, it's eleven on a Wednesday morning, six weeks into my New York trip. Leo and I are planning on staying even longer—the director wants Leo's help with postproduction and editing here, when they're done shooting. They'll be cutting the show in New York, taking advantage of a brand-new tax break, and I'm going to stay with him.

"Christmas in Brooklyn," Leo said to me this weekend. Sunday, drinking lattes at East One Coffee Roasters, the place we're now regulars, and sharing avocado toast and chorizo hash. A walk down Flatbush to pick up bagels. Takeout from SHAN on Smith Street.

"Sounds perfect," I said.

The longer we spend in New York the better it feels. To start something new, away from the beach. To begin again. Holiday windows, hot chocolate, and ice-skating in Central Park. I feel New York like a romance novel. I just keep turning the pages.

We have even started talking about maybe moving here, maybe giving up West Hollywood entirely and renting something— temporary, to start. Work is paying for Leo through the New Year, and after that, if the show gets picked up for a second season . . . it might all make sense.

I pick up on the third ring. I don't think anything of it. It's 8:00 a.m. in Los Angeles. It's a Wednesday. It's a perfectly reasonable time to call your only daughter for no reason at all.

"Mom," I say. "Hey, what's up?"

I'm already thinking that I'll stop by Sweetgreen for lunch, and pick up some stuff for dinner at Union Market—maybe a few pieces of salmon to grill and some of their marinated cauliflower. It's overpriced, but worth it. On the nights Leo has late shoots I've been taking myself to a wine bar around the corner and posting up at a table with my laptop, but tonight I'm craving some time inside. A good book, maybe a *Housewives* season, and a fresh summer salad to go along with it.

"Where are you?" she asks me, and I know immediately that something is wrong.

"What happened?"

"It's Dad," she says. "He's in the hospital."

Immediately I think accident, but I can tell from her tone that's not it. She doesn't have the harried voice of someone pacing outside the ER, waiting for a blood transfusion to work, in triage. Rather, she sounds like someone who is staving off a very heavy reality from setting in.

"Why?" I ask.

I hear her inhale. "I'd rather you come home," she says.

I imagine all the steps I need to take to get back there. Calling the airlines, packing, Uber, flight. I'm at least fifteen hours away from an answer.

"I need to know what's going on," I say. "Mom, tell me. What's happening with Dad?"

"It's his heart," she says, and her voice cracks.

I feel panic mixed with anger. The hot-blooded annoyance at my mom, her hand-wringing, her singular focus on my father's health, life, person. Of course it's his heart. It's always been his heart.

"What about it?"

"He had an episode," she says.

"What kind of episode? A heart attack? Mom, use your words."

"A heart attack."

"Who said that? The doctors? Did they confirm that? Let me talk to him."

"Lauren!" She screams it through the phone.

I go silent. I hear her breathing on the other end of the line.

"Honey," she says. She so rarely calls me that. I can't even remember the last time. "I think you need to come home now."

I call Leo and it goes straight to voicemail. I go online and book a flight for this afternoon; I'll be home in time for dinner in LA. Cedars is forty-five minutes from LAX. I start throwing things into a carry-on—toothbrush, T-shirt, a pack of hair ties.

I text my mom my flight information. She likes it. Thumbs-up.

I need to go back to LA. Dad is in the hospital. I don't know details. I'll call you when I land. I love you.

The plane ride seems both short and endless. Two hours becomes six, but then we are landing in Los Angeles. My cell phone bars come and go, come and go, as we make our descent.

There are no new messages from Mom, and then—

Text me when you land.

I do immediately—resentful, still, of her tone. Of her withholding. *Just fucking tell me.* And, yikes: *Why is everything such a big fucking deal?*

We're on the cardio floor. Ask for Dr. Berk, comes the reply.

I text Leo: *Landed. Call when you can.*

I'm walking out to meet the Uber when my phone rings. It's him. "Babe, tell me. What's going on?"

"I landed. Going straight to the hospital."

"Did you talk to them? I called; she didn't answer."

"No, not yet. She keeps being very cagey. You know my mom."

Leo makes a noncommittal noise.

"She's scared," he says.

His words hit me. He's defending her. Or, no, he's trying to prepare me.

"Yeah, well."

"You'll call me from the hospital?"

"Of course."

Leo is quiet for a moment. "Hang in there. I'll be out as soon as I can."

He hangs up before I can protest, before I can tell him that there's no need. This is just a speed bump. Dad will be *fine*. I'll come back to New York; we'll pick up this summer of freedom right where we left it off.

My Uber and I manage to choose each other correctly, and then we are speeding out of Terminal 7 in search of the freeway. My phone rings again. I think it's Leo, calling to tell me he's going to get the next flight, or my mom saying she's overreacted, the doctor just came in and actually everything is looking just fine. . . .

But it's none of those things, of course it isn't.

Stone is calling.

I hold the phone in my fingertips. I can feel my hands start to shake.

The staccato beats of my ringtone formulate another verse.

I curl my lip over my teeth and answer.

CHAPTER TWENTY-SEVEN

She hates hospitals, but doesn't everyone hate hospitals? The lights, the staccato beeping, the impending, hovering reality of death. Yes, everyone hates hospitals, but people have different levels of tolerance for the things they hate. Marcella has little.

She paces outside her husband's room. Her mother sits inside with him, chattering on about something to do with the house. He is awake, conscious, lucid. But he is not well. The disconnect between these things—his appearance, the reality—is not hard for her to grasp. She is used to the power of invisible things.

The doctors have told her the reality she has feared for the past thirty years has come to pass—his heart, in its current configuration, is giving out. After his open-heart surgery, way back in this very same hospital, they created bypasses. Two of those bypasses closed over the years, but he has been kept alive by a series of small capillaries—God's bypasses, the doctor called them. The body's response to needing a route to the heart. But now they are being impacted—whether because his liver is not as good at breaking down fat as before or because the concoction of medications has stopped being as effective, they are not sure. Regardless, it's a hard situation to operate on. These bypasses are little—not the ones they replaced years ago but much, much smaller. They are a miracle, the doctor has told her. But even miracles have expiration dates.

It had been a normal day. Nothing particular to write home about. He hadn't gone surfing, but she knew. The truth is there was little she did not know. She knew that he snuck regular coffee, not decaf, into the cannister and that he didn't change the pillowcases when he said he did. She knew all of these things already. Why hadn't she said anything? Why hadn't she insisted they visit the cardiologist earlier than their annual? The truth is, she didn't want to know because knowing would make it true.

All he did was come up the stairs.

She saw him sway from the window at the sink. At first she thought he was being silly, playful—interpretive dance on the water, listening to the music in his own head—but then she saw him fall.

He was lucky. He was close to the sand, and there was a pile of beach towels on the bottom step. Dave still brought them down for the surfers, for anyone who came out of the water and needed a little warmth. Sometimes they'd stay down for days, getting damp and crunchy from the salt water. She'd ask him to bring them up so she could wash them, but he always forgot.

They broke his fall.

She called 911 before she even stepped outside. They told her to do CPR, but she didn't remember how. She had learned, of course. In all the years of worrying, of hospitals and doctors and medications, she had taken the course. But she never thought she'd have to use it, not really. She couldn't remember if it was eight pumps or six. She couldn't remember if it was on the breastbone or below.

Please, she said. *Just come.*

She started screaming. Down the beach at whoever could hear. Maybe someone knew how to turn back time. Maybe someone else had a ticket they hadn't yet spent. That's the truth—it took almost no time for her to know she was out of cards. She didn't think about it down the road—minutes or hours later. She thought about it instantly. She thought about it while she still believed he was kidding. *If. When. I have no way to save you.*

Now she is in his hospital room. Sylvia laughs, and Marcella turns away. She knows that Lauren thinks her feelings toward her mother are warranted, understandable. Lauren does not know that Marcella resents her, too. She resents the obvious ease of Lauren's life—two parents, a healthy husband, a second chance.

She thinks about her daughter then, earlier, again, than she'd like to admit. She thinks about her in the hospital, and she thinks about her on those steps, before the towels break her beloved husband's fall. She thinks about her ticket. She knows that it is unused.

She waits to call Lauren. She waits until she knows what is happening. Until he does not die but instead wakes up in a hospital room, tethered to a bed. A cardiac arrest. A damaged aortic valve. A blocked artery. No possibility of a stent, not anymore. She waits, but she already knows. She calls her daughter because this is her father, she needs to inform her—of course, of course. She calls her daughter because Lauren has the one thing Marcella does not and can't get back.

Time.

CHAPTER TWENTY-EIGHT

In the back of the Uber headed to Cedars-Sinai, I clear my throat and press the receiver to my ear.

"Hi."

"Lauren, hi. Wow. It's been a long time."

I let myself for the first time think about the parking lot six weeks ago. I think about the flip of the driver's seat, the sharp edge of the metal belt. Stone's hands and words. All the things I erased.

"Yeah, hi. I heard about Bonnie. I'm so glad the trial is working."

"Oh." He pauses. "It's . . . we got another few weeks, but ultimately things took a turn. The doctors say that happens sometimes. There's a rebound and then . . ."

I feel my hands go numb. I switch the phone to the other ear.

"When did that happen?" I say.

"About two weeks ago, maybe three, it's hard to keep track. She's not doing so good, Laur."

I close my eyes against the sound of my nickname in his mouth. One tragedy at a time.

"I'm so sorry."

"Yeah, me, too. Listen, where are you?"

I squint out the window. We are crawling along the 405.

"LA," I say. "Just landed. My dad is in the hospital."

"Shit, I'm sorry. I haven't seen him out the past few mornings, I was wondering what was up. He comes down most mornings, even to just bring the guys coffee and towels."

"Yeah, well, now you know."

We are silent for a moment. My eyes start to burn, and I close them. I close them against the rising tide, against this feeling of my father—generous and kind. Present. Here.

"Why are you calling?" I ask.

"I went to the Greek the other night and thought of you." I hear his breath through the phone. It comes in low hums. "I guess with everything going on I just wanted to hear your voice."

I see us there, feet over the edge of the deck, in the quiet dark. I see him taking my hand.

Does he remember, somehow? Does he know?

"Oh," I say, because it was so long ago that we were connected, so long ago that he would think to reach out to me. When was the last time we were alone, for him? Eight years? Ten?

I think about Stone in the car. Stone saying, "I never should have left." Does he believe that? Or was that only true that night, in that car, unclothed? Was it only true because of everything that led up to it?

I push the memory away. Because it isn't a memory. Something can't be a memory if it never actually happened.

"What's going on with Dave?" he asks. I can hear the concern in his voice.

"It's his heart," I say. "I don't know much. My mom called while I was in New York, and I got the next flight."

Traffic starts to move now, like the flush after an acupuncture treatment. Open channels.

"I should go," I say, before he can respond to what came before.

"Yeah, no, of course."

"I'm so sorry about Bonnie." And then, "This isn't my place, but you should give her morphine. I know she doesn't want it, but you should anyway."

Stone doesn't say anything; I just hear him inhale.

It seems impossible that this is happening, again. That she has to go through this, again. For a moment I wonder if I've inadvertently gifted her two declines, two deaths. Two sufferings.

"Where are you going to stay while you're here?" he asks quietly. Finally.

I remember our place is rented, of course it is.

"The beach," I say, as we merge right toward La Cienega Boulevard.

CHAPTER TWENTY-NINE

Cedars-Sinai is the third-leading cardiology hospital in all of the United States. It ranks only behind Cleveland Clinic and the Mayo Clinic. Its offices are filled with award-winning research doctors and surgeons. But it is still a hospital. The staff is overworked; the waiting rooms are oozing with sick people; the paint is chipped. There isn't enough—money, resources, time.

I check in downstairs to be told that I've showed up in the middle of rounds. I will have to wait for them to call up to the nurses' station. My father is on the cardio floor, not the ICU—a good sign, I think. I step into the driveway and call my mom.

"Hi, where are you?"

"Downstairs," I say. "They said I have to wait for nurses' rounds to be done."

"I'll come down."

She hangs up, and I shoot off another text to Leo.

At hospital. Waiting to be let up.

The elevator doors open and out step a variety of colored scrubs, a young man pushing an older man in a wheelchair, and my mother.

She looks smaller than she usually does, thinner, and it's this that hits me first. Not her call, not the hospital, not him being here, but her physical form.

I go over to her. She gives me a tight hug.

"Let me just talk to them," she says, gesturing toward the help desk.

She goes over and exchanges a few words with the same mid-thirties man who helped me. This time the man smiles and nods his head toward me. I hand over my ID and am printed a name sticker.

"You're all set," he says.

I follow Marcella back to the elevators. When they close us inside we are, miraculously, alone.

"How is he doing?" I ask.

"Pretty good," she says. "We just saw the doctor. He says we have to make a decision about how to move forward."

"What does that mean?"

"It means his heart is weak right now. It's not getting enough blood."

The doors open. The cardio floor is calm but buzzing, Nurses move in and out of rooms and around one another. Phones at the station ring. I suddenly realize how unprepared for this I am. How woefully ignorant I've been. How could I have questioned her? How could I not have raced here even sooner? Run across the country on my two bare feet?

"He's in here," Marcella says, and her tone is soft, kind. She sounds like my mom.

She peels back the curtain, and there Dad is, low in bed, the machines beeping, low and slow.

"Dad," I whisper, and he stirs.

He's not sitting up, not all the way, but he's not lying down, either. When I take another two steps inside, I can see his face.

"He's OK," my mom says. The first cheerful thing she's said to me since that phone call, and I know it's for his benefit. She smiles, tight and even, as I move closer. In another two steps, I'm at his bedside.

There are wires in his veins and under his nose, and his hair is flat to his face, the result of no showers, no product, but other than that he looks like Dad.

He opens his eyes and smiles lightly at me. Happy I'm here. Unsurprised.

"Honey," he says softly.

"Hey, Dad." I feel my throat constrict. "How are you?"

"Been better," he says, but the first word gets swallowed so all that comes out is *better*.

"You're doing good," my mom says. She goes to the other side, smooths the hair off his forehead. I notice some stray iodine on his cheek. "We are just waiting for Dr. Gupta to tell us what he thinks."

"They want to open me up again," Dad says to me. His words get stronger and clearer the more he speaks. "You heard that."

I look at my mom. I feel, all at once, like I don't want to betray her. "We should listen to the doctors," I say.

"Not again," Dad says. "Not this time."

My mother closes the curtain. She comes back and takes his hand. "Let's be calm," she says, stroking his palm. "We will do whatever we need to do, OK?"

And then she looks at me. It's brief, just her eyes, not her face. A flicker. But I know what she's saying. All at once, I understand what she's asking of me. The reason she is not caught in the details. She is hoping they won't matter.

I don't have it, I think, and the realization sends me sailing backward. But there's nowhere to go, of course, because it's gone. Evaporated, like the moments before it. There is only here. This hospital. This room.

The relentless present.

"Mom," I say. "Let's let Dad rest."

"I'm fine," he says. "This is all a bit dramatic."

"No," Marcella says. "Close your eyes. We'll be right back."

She grabs her bag off the chair and takes my elbow, pivoting me toward the door.

CHAPTER THIRTY

We sit in hard plastic chairs in the cafeteria that smells like hospital. All around us, nurses and doctors, staff and patients, line up for coffee or packaged sandwiches, tiny tins of fruit. How anyone could ingest anything in here is beyond me. It's impossible to have an appetite when sour air is being pumped through the vents.

My stomach has turned outside in.

"I want to get back up there," Marcella says.

"I don't have it," I say.

If she doesn't have time, I won't waste ours.

Marcella looks at me. Blinks slowly.

"I used it. Recently. Something happened that I needed—" I don't want to explain myself, because I'm ashamed of what I'd have to say, the childish and embarrassing turn I took. "I used it."

I have very rarely seen Marcella angry. Even when I was a child, she never raised her voice.

But now—

"How could you?" she says.

She doesn't move, doesn't stand, but it's like her whole body begins to tower.

I see a rage in her that is entirely unfamiliar and yet intimately known, because it is the same one I have. It's the rage that has burned in me every day since the accident, since I lost her to the idea of his safety. The rage at being second place. At being this scared, this careful.

"I'm sorry," I say, but I'm not. I feel glad I used it, in this moment. I want to punish her. I feel selfish and wild. I want her to know that what I've done I've done for me. "It was mine, and I used it because I wanted to." And then, as if throwing it away. "No one told me Dad needed it."

But of course that is not true. I knew. I've always known. That someday, probably, we'd end up here. I was saving it for him, wasn't I? If I'm honest? I believed, all those years, that it was my duty. When I saw him out on the deck, struggling with the board, I knew. That he was alive because of my mom and that he'd stay alive because of me. And then I spared my husband's heart instead.

"I thought for sure—" my mother says. She is clenching and unclenching her fists. "I thought for sure you *understood*."

"Why?" I say. "You just assumed what's mine would be yours when you needed it again?"

I see something in my mother turn over. The anger dissolves into sadness. Right in front of me, right in the middle of this hospital cafeteria it melts, loses form. In another moment the table is dripping with it. "I hoped—"

"That I'd save Dad just like you did. That I was meant to."

There it is, between us. The thing we've never said. Years of guilt and grief woven like an umbilical cord between us. The truth that we are nothing without him.

"No," she says. "I hoped he'd never need it."

She stands up then. Pushes in her chair. I lift my coffee to my lips. Let her go, get back upstairs. She has no more need for me, anyway.

"I'm going to stay down here," I say. "Tell Dad. Or don't."

She is standing behind her chair. She looks at me, and I feel my face mirrored in hers. I never thought I looked much like my mother—no one did. I was squarely Dave Novak's child. But sitting here now I feel her expressions running through me like marionette strings.

"I'm not going upstairs," she says.

I cross my arms; I just keep staring at her. I feel my petulance losing its footing. A dusty hillside.

"Stand up," she tells me. "You're coming with me."

CHAPTER THIRTY-ONE

My story does not begin here, but if this is the time allotted, I'll take it. *Begin as you mean to go on*, they say, but I've always felt that *go on as you began* is the more helpful idiom. None of us need help at the beginning. And the end is going to come no matter whose hands are there. Where we might require aid is the middle, where the meat is.

But I digress. After all, this is not my story.

This is not my middle, either. This is, by all accounts, my end. When you are in your nineties, the facts speak for themselves. There is only so long one can stay at the fair, so to speak. Eventually, the rides stop, the vendors close up shop. We get the time we get and no more.

I am nearing the final bend, rounding the penultimate corner. There cannot possibly be that much time left, and yet—time is a funny thing. At this point I feel confident in saying our measuring device is incomplete. We don't take it all into consideration.

My daughter once told me that no time is promised. When she said it I was in my seventies and it felt like the end then, too, I suppose. Who could have seen these twenty years coming. But my daughter was wrong. Time is promised. But not to us. Time is promised to the earth. We are merely its inhabitants. We are not owed anything.

In the eighties, on a trip to Morocco, a woman I met in our riad said the following to me: *Being alive is everything. Anything beyond that is pure gravy.* We were on mushrooms, but the point stands.

At this stage all I've got is words. There are no more tits, no waist. I'd put on makeup if I could still locate my eyelids. Getting old it not for the faint of heart, and anyone who tells you differently is thirty-fucking-five.

I was raised in New York, in a town outside the city called Scarsdale. My mother, Irina, came to the US when she was just eight years old, with nothing but a small trunk and her mother. Her father was a cobbler—well, you know that already—and sad to say he never made it to the shores. When they docked in the city it was just her and her mother, who wasn't much of a help at all. Her father had run the show, and now that he was gone, my mother was in charge. Irina moved in with family. Her mother's sister had come before and was sharing an apartment in Brooklyn. Irina and her mother slept in the living room.

Everyone in the building went to work. And everyone in the building had shoes. And soon Irina had started a nice little business. She'd mend and make whatever the needs of the building were for half of what any shop would charge. Word spread, and soon everyone in the neighborhood came to her. She had more work than she could handle—the apartment was filled with shoes—and so she opened her own shop. It was a small place on the corner of Flatbush and Avenue D, and soon Irina and her mother moved into the apartment above. All day and all night Irina did what her father taught her. And with her own two hands, she built a new life.

My father was a customer. They'd known each other since they were children. He'd bring in the family's shoes, and she'd work on them. Sometimes he'd bring her a nickel sandwich from Juniors or a small pot of kasha and bow ties from his mother's kitchen. Morris brought his family's shoes in to be shined more than was sensible, Irina knew that, but as they turned from children to teens she looked forward to his visits with a different kind of enthusiasm.

Like all the young men in the neighborhood, Morris left to serve in the war, and when he came back he asked Irina to marry him. They spent twenty-eight years married, and he died at fifty-two after a short battle with liver cancer.

I never asked my mother if she regretted her choice—saving her father, only to have him leave them so soon after. Whether she longed for the decades she spent alone after her husband's death to be different. I never asked, because I knew it was the wrong question. To long for things to be different is to fundamentally miss the lesson of life. My mother taught me that, and while we were not close, I had a lot of respect for her. Her practicality, her tenacity, the way she built a life here on her own skill and back. I never forgot it, and when I think of her, even now—so very often, it is always with reverence.

To put it pleasantly, life is a bit of a game. A sport. It's hard, and you can make it harder, easy for no one, and the only way out is through. I'm an old lady, so if this rambles, please blame my age. Not my hesitation, never. I'm still trying to figure out how to tell you.

You want to know what became of my ticket. Or rather, how I used it. You have to understand that I had it since I was born—ninety-one years. I knew about it for at least eighty-five. That's a lot of time. I have made so many mistakes. We all have, but I've made more than my fair share. I left my baby in the care of my mother to live in Finland with a rock star. I ruined a marriage. Well, three of them, and none of them mine. Richard, Cash, and John. I loved them all. I was engaged four times, and married none. I regretted things, of course. I lost my patience with my daughter. I was erratic with strangers. Once, I slapped a man on the street for touching a woman's ass who happened to be his wife.

I was arrested twice, both for disturbing the peace. I marched with Martin Luther King Jr. and protested the war and, despite living at the ocean, never really learned how to swim. Or taught my daughter.

I broke my leg after I was thrown from my horse, Penny, and never got back on. I once told a woman in the ladies' room of Musso & Frank that her husband was running around on her. I had the wrong guy. I lit Shabbat candles every Friday the first year of my daughter's life and then never again.

I don't have many friends, but I've met almost everyone.

Do you see where this is going, my dear?

CHAPTER THIRTY-TWO

She takes her daughter out of the hospital doors and down the long corridor, toward the elevators that lead to the parking structure.

She remembers then the wild ride to the hospital, thirty-seven years ago, the way Dave kept white-knuckling the steering wheel, screaming at the top of his lungs: *Hold on!* She laughed between contractions, told him to calm down. But he couldn't calm down—this was it; their baby was coming. She would be born five short hours later, after only fifteen minutes of pushing, rocketing into the world ahead of schedule. Marcella had been warned that first children normally come late, but Lauren had been a whole three days early. She was ready to be here.

Marcella remembers the wild screech into the valet area—complete with sound effects—and the way Dave hollered at the parking attendant that his wife was in labor.

"Parking Structure A," the woman said, unfazed. Hadn't been her first overly excited husband.

Marcella clutched her stomach as they made their way to labor and delivery. The contractions were coming hard and fast, and she knew what that meant—she knew her daughter was nearly there.

Marcella was never close with Sylvia. In some ways, she thought, it was impossible to be. Her mother was gone often, preferring her own world over the one she could occupy at home. She wasn't cold, but she wasn't exactly warm, either. She was loud and opinionated and excited, but not warm. Marcella had almost no memories of being held before Dave. And she wants to change all that with her daughter. With the birth of this baby, Marcella believes she has the ability to do it over, to have the kind of mother-daughter relationship she had always longed for. She promised herself, as the fire ran across her belly, that she would be there, that she would do it differently. That every milestone, every memory, would be together.

"Push!!"

Marcella held the plastic edge of the hospital bed, sweating and screaming. Dave pressed a cool compress to her head. There hadn't been time for an epidural, and she felt pulled in two, like her actual insides were about to rip, were ripping, and still they were screaming for more.

"I can't," she said.

Dave leaned down close. Usually his presence was a comfort to her, a balm. Just a hug could calm her nervous system. But now she felt like he was sucking what little oxygen she had left.

Still they told her to push. Did they not see her trying? If she'd had a lick of energy she would have told them to care more about her, about the woman right in front of them, but she couldn't speak.

She screamed out something guttural, a sound she knew for certain she had never made before, knew for certain she had likely never heard before.

And then, there she was. All seven pounds nine ounces of her. She was wet and slippery and red and bruised and there.

Marcella and Lauren reach the ramp that leads up to Parking Structure A.

"What are we doing?" Lauren says. She checks her watch. She appears agitated.

Marcella wants to put her arms around her daughter, to shake her, to look into her eyes and make her see. *Don't you understand?*

That was the day she was born. Marcella remembers it all clearly, exactly. Just like it were yesterday.

But Marcella did not bring her daughter here today to tell her about the day she was born.

She brought her here to tell her about the day she died.

CHAPTER THIRTY-THREE

We're standing at Alden Drive, a few paces over from the emergency entrance to the hospital. Cars pull in and out of the cul-de-sac, dropping off and picking up patients. It's less chaotic than you'd think, being the emergency entrance to the biggest hospital in Los Angeles. No sirens, no whirling ambulances. Just the slow stream in and out of sick people.

Marcella is clutching and uncurling her hands in repetition. She's wearing khaki pants and a black sweater and Reebok sneakers, and she looks, all at once, old—older than I remember. My mother has always been youthful and vibrant, if uptight. Rarely a wrinkle, petite and tight body. But I see her now, not as young as before. The realization feels cruel, somehow—and I'm immediately filled with regret. At my attitude in the cafeteria. At being angry with her when really I am angry at myself.

But I want her to know what this summer has been like. I want her to know that it *worked*.

"I had a second chance," I tell her. Still angry, still kicking, but the truth.

A Honda drives by with the radio blaring nineties rap. We both turn to look as it whizzes by.

"Yes, well—"

"No, Mom. For real. I did something bad. Something bad to Leo and—"

But then I feel it, the injustice of it. The thing I keep buried down deep inside my heart. The thing I've sworn to Leo we will let go of. The thing I've "given up." The absolute garbage, the utter infuriating impossibility, that I cannot get pregnant.

And all at once I want to tell her. I want Marcella to know. Because she doesn't, she has no idea what we—*I*—have been going through. The hormones and the drugs and the utter despair that, once again, it did not work. That once again, another month—another year—has gone by and there is no child in our arms.

"I can't have a baby," I say. I say it plainly, but it feels like screaming. The declaration feels like the only thing that has ever been spoken aloud in the whole world.

Marcella blinks at me. "What do you mean?"

"I mean I can't get pregnant. We've been trying for three years. We've done every fertility treatment under the sun, many times over. And none of it works."

I'm angry, and I'm angry at her, at her obliviousness, at her insistence that life should be and is orderly. That people meet and fall in love and have a child and that marriage is uncomplicated and that motherhood is given. That she's never noticed before, the gaping hole in her daughter's life. That every time I'm over for Shabbat after a failed retrieval or visiting for the weekend after my period comes that she hasn't seen my eyes, that she's never asked me what's wrong and really, truly, wanted to know.

"Oh, honey," she says. "I had no idea."

We stare at each other for a brief moment that feels charged—the anger, the recognition. We are strangers to each other. We have no idea about the other's life.

"This summer," I say, "I cheated on Leo. He went to New York, and I came to the beach, and I slept with Stone."

I see Marcella react, but I push on.

"Things have been hard. We needed money for fertility; Leo didn't want to keep going; I was angry with his absence. Being with Stone made me feel like . . . like maybe I wasn't broken."

My mother says nothing, just keeps looking at me.

"And then I took it back, and it was like we had a second chance." The tears come fast, now. Fluid and hot. "And we weren't just grieving anymore, we were happy. Really, truly happy. We gave up and we got our marriage back."

Marcella opens her mouth to protest, to say, maybe, some inane thing they all say: *Don't give up. Don't worry, it'll happen. When you least except it. You just have to believe; miracles happen all the time.*

But for some women, they don't. For some women there is no miracle, no spontaneous pregnancy, no twelfth retrieval where, finally, the One Good Egg, the end. For some women there is only the big, open, wide, gaping middle.

"It felt great. It worked. The do-over worked. It made everything better."

"I know," Marcella says. "Sweetheart, I understand."

I look at her. I see now that she's crying. Big tears falling down her cheeks. I realize how infrequently I've ever seen my mother cry, how infrequently I've ever seen her *moved*.

"I got a second chance," I say. "And now—"

Marcella, my mother, looks at me. She takes a deep breath. I see her get quiet, very quiet. And then she puts her hands on my shoulders. She holds them there. She looks into my eyes, and it's like I see it before she says it, like I know, just from looking.

"It has all been a second chance," she says, and then she tells me.

CHAPTER THIRTY-FOUR

She knows exactly where to start because she has practiced this identical conversation hundreds of times in her head. She has run and rerun the dialogue, the tilt of her head, the flow and rhythm of her words.

Of course, there are details that are different—it being here and now. There are the heightened circumstances surrounding this moment—the hospital, the parking structure, the sound of an ambulance. Her husband, above them, somewhere. But even these, in a way, have been accounted for. There was never going to be an ordinary utterance of this narrative. It was always going to be told under duress.

She begins, as she always knew she would, with the call. Dave, on his cell phone. One of those big, wide, flip phones they had in the early 2000s. She, Marcella, didn't have a cell phone back then. She was a late adopter, refusing new technology. There wasn't even a beeper in her bag.

"Oh, I could never work that," she'd tell Dave.

So the home phone rang. It was 6:00 p.m. Dave and Lauren were coming back from a volleyball game. Malibu High had been playing Harvard-Westlake in Beverly Hills. She had packed orange slices for the team. Lauren loved oranges.

"Mar," he said—his voice shaking, broken, breakable—"there's been an accident."

She knew, all at once, that it was serious. That her daughter was not OK. She knew in the way mothers always know—even the ones who feel like strangers to their children.

"Where is she?"

"We're on our way to Cedars," he said. "Honey, it's not good."

She remembers that he sounded like a little boy. That he was not her athletic, strong, strapping husband but someone who needed her care. That he was *terrified*. She grabbed her keys, and ran.

She did ninety down the PCH, and to this day she remembers nothing about the drive here, nor leaving her car, abandoned in this same space somewhere.

"My daughter," she puffed out at the help desk. "She's here; she's injured."

"Name?"

"Lauren Novak."

The woman looked up at her. Did she have the information? She swore, she could see it there, written on her sad, practiced face.

"She's in surgery," she said. "Someone will come and get you."

"I can't wait," she said. "I'm her mother."

She was screaming.

"Ma'am, I'm sorry, I'm going to need to ask you to wait."

She paced for what felt like hours. In reality it was three minutes and twelve seconds. A woman came out in scrubs.

"Mrs. Novak?"

Marcella followed the nurse down the corridor through beeping machines and movement and lights and one man's loud, desperate moans. She ended up at Dave.

He stood from the chair in the small waiting room—the bereavement room, she later realized—in full hysterics. He was not stunned or stoic or panicked. He was in full, loud, messy grief.

"Mar," he said, through unencumbered sobs. "She's gone. She's gone."

He collapsed into her, his wife, her mother. He collapsed into her as if she could save him and her. As if she could bring her back.

There was no way. No. Just no. She screamed it. She shoved her husband back. Her savior, her safe space. The man she married and called her home. He had betrayed her. He had been the one at the wheel.

No.

She screamed it until it became unintelligible. Until it wasn't a word, a single syllable, but a guttural roar. It sounded like the day Lauren was born, she realized. Birth and death.

Sometime later Sylvia showed up. Dave was making arrangements—she couldn't think about what that word meant, really.

In her telling, Sylvia was calm, collected. But in reality that is not completely true, and Marcella corrects herself now. "Memory is fiction, of course," she tells her daughter. "Especially for those of us who get to revise it."

No, Sylvia was not calm. She felt heavy, even to Marcella, in the thick of her own shock and grief. Marcella could feel her mother's weight. For many years she believed that the heaviness was her own grief—her beloved granddaughter—who Marcella suspected, no, knew, she loved more than her own daughter. At least understood more, cared for more. But that was not it, not completely. What Sylvia oozed was inevitability. It was the point she herself had dreaded, the way Marcella has dreaded this one, standing with Lauren at the entrance to Parking Structure A.

The truth, finally.

"There's a way," Sylvia said, and that was that.

Marcella stares at Lauren. She has tried to say this gently, but there is only so lightly one can set down the truth. It's going to make a sound no matter the fingertips.

"It was you, honey," Marcella says to her.

She can see her daughter trying to digest this, trying to reorder the past in her own mind so that the new narrative slots in, but of course, it isn't an easy switch. It isn't simply Dave's death for her own but a full reorienting of their family narrative, their collective trauma, as it were. What does it mean if Dave wasn't saved? What does it mean that he never needed it, not until now?

"Why did you never tell me?" Lauren wants to know.

And this one is easy. Marcella exhales out the breath she has been holding.

"Because," she says. "I'm your mother. It has always been my job to protect you."

CHAPTER THIRTY-FIVE

There, on the street, as a blue Nissan Pathfinder pulls into the lot, I feel the world lift. Like the trees, grass, concrete underground are all peeling themselves up up up, away from gravity. They hover, up there, in the air, and then they slowly begin to turn. Ten, fifteen, twenty, forty, ninety degrees. Everything now faces north when before it was east.

Now looking at a new horizon, things click back down into place. And it's only when I feel the sidewalk underneath me once again, the cars honking nearby, the call of a father up the street that I understand that this was always supposed to be where we were.

No. We were always here.

I look at Marcella. She has tears streaming down her face, but for the first time I feel like I can really see her. Not because she saved me, but because she is telling the truth about her story—and the truth is always the shortest distance between two points. Here the two points stand, outside a hospital, meeting, finally.

"I love you," she says. "My life started the day you were born and started over again the day you lived."

I think about that day in my room, my mother and Sylvia sitting me down. Marcella had pivoted. She had replaced the truth because what kind of woman tells their fifteen-year-old daughter that she has just died?

"But what about Dad?" I ask.

And now I see it—why she was always so worried about him. It wasn't because she had saved him once before. It was because she never had, because she knew about his heart, knew what might be coming for him, and was already aware that there would be nothing she could do to stop it. It was the worry we all have—the worry of the unknown. The worry of what it means to be human, to love someone, to be powerless in the face of it.

"Dad knew, too," she says. "He told me to tell you so many times. He said I'd get you off his back." She laughs. "But he knew it was my choice to make."

Hysterical strength, the term used to address the phenomenon of the adrenaline mothers get when their children are in danger. The superhuman capabilities these women uncover. The mom who lifted a car off her baby, who scaled a building to save her toddler. What was the ticket if not hysterical strength? What has our life been if not that?

"I'm sorry you had to carry this," I say, and when I do I see her body crumple. She pitches forward, and I catch her in my arms—my mother. She folds into me, and I hold her, and once her body is pressed against mine, once we are connected, in ways we haven't been in so long, I feel myself give way, too. And it's there in the passage—mother and child, child and mother, grief and love and love and grief, the indistinguishable nature of these things, their inherent ties, that I finally understand the legacy I come from.

We are saviors.

What does it mean that I chose—selfishly, hastily, thoughtlessly—to save myself?

CHAPTER THIRTY-SIX

When I was twenty-nine I met a man on a trip to Las Vegas. Bobby Montgomery. A cowboy from Kentucky with a Southern drawl and biceps built like a bison.

We fell in love almost immediately. I don't use that term lightly. I'm old, and I have no reason to lie anymore, to narrate my life in any way other than what it was. Love, yes. I had never felt it the way I felt it for him, and nothing later came close, either—although there was a split for second place a mile long.

It was Sin City back then, and the whole town dripped with devil-may-care. The mob still ran the town, and Lefty ran the desk at the International. I used to gamble, play the slots. Tables, too. My family wonders where the money comes from, and the truth is no one ever made a living at blackjack but me. Fifty thousand dollars in 1964 can become ten million by 2020 without too much effort. All I ever bought was the house, and the rest just got to grow.

But back to Bobby.

The Rat Pack—Frank and Sammy and Dean—called the shots right along with the Family. Elvis had just come out with "Viva Las Vegas," and people were pilgriming in droves. I already knew I had a knack for the tables—call it luck, intuition, who knows.

Mostly it was bravery. I had the silver ticket, you see. Any mistake I made, any bad thing that happened, I could take it back. I was invincible. I lived without fear.

"Excuse me, miss, you seem to have dropped something."

He appeared at my side, all six feet four inches of him, with a cowboy hat tipped forward on his head and his palm outstretched. I was at the Trop—not staying there, too rich for my blood—but posted up at the Theatre Restaurant. It was the see and be seen of 1964.

The something I had dropped, apparently, was his hand.

Bobby was in town working a slot route—he'd been hooked up with Phil Kastel somewhere in Louisiana and was in Vegas seeing the fruits of his friend's new venture.

We became inseparable. He had a suite with two rooms and offered me the second, but by our third night it was obvious—there really wasn't a need for more than the one.

I'd had sex before. I was an unmarried woman in the fifties, which was a tough thing to be if you were anyone else, but I'd grown up with a mother who left me to my own devices.

Bobby and I fell fast. The Little White Chapel had been built in 1954 and he asked me to go.

"Little lady, won't you be my bride?"

I was a Jewish girl with a Ukrainian mother, and he was a Southern heir with one dead father, and together, we were an absurdity—but dear, did I want to.

We spent four and a half months all over the strip. Dinner at Louigi's, Golden Steer Steakhouse to hear Sinatra grab the mic after two martinis. It was like living in a movie. I knew, even in it, how rare the air was. I loved every minute of it.

It was the closest I ever came to being married, but in the end, there just wasn't enough time.

Kastel was getting pushed out of the casino because of his connections to mob boss Frank Costello. I was worried Bobby would get caught in the crosshairs. Carlos Marcello was taking over, and he didn't like anyone who was left from the old regime. That was Bobby.

It was a Friday morning. I remember because I was going to tell him that night at dinner—our Shabbat. I was going to light candles in the room and order up the chicken and open some nice Scotch.

I had suspected it for a week or two and then called the doctor to confirm. An old guy who went by Dr. Sam and came to the room.

"You're about two months along," he told me. I'd been in Las Vegas eighteen weeks.

Bobby never came back for dinner. He didn't come back the next night, either. It was Sunday before I went downstairs and asked for Kastel. No one knew. Then I went and found Lefty.

"He's gone," Lefty said. He worked the International but he knew it all, everything that went down on the strip. "You don't want to know a lot more."

I never found out what happened, although I suspect I knew. He was killed, dumped the way they all were. There were no news stories that would come out, no cell phones. I had nothing but a name.

I told myself if I didn't hear from him in a month, I'd use it. I'd turn the clock back and I'd be with him again. I'd tell him I'd make sure we never parted. But a month went by, and then I felt her kick for the first time—my feisty, fiery, fierce baby.

I went to Los Angeles. I didn't know where else to go. Bobby had been generous, in those few brief months, and I had a nice stash of cash. What was left in the room—plenty, more than you can imagine, for those days—I took, too.

I was pulled out to Malibu—by fate or destiny or just the smell of the ocean, I'm not sure. There was nothing much along Point Dume then—a couple of houses. The Colony was already buzzing with movie stars, and Gidget was riding the waves at Surfrider Beach.

I had enough for the down payment in cash. An architect had built the home two years prior and had never intended to keep it. The house was too big for me—I knew that—but I needed somewhere to be, somewhere to put myself and this child—and the beach seemed as good a place as any.

Marcella came screaming into the world at home the following summer. She had a mess of curly straw-colored hair at birth and Bobby's bright green eyes, and I loved her with a ferocity I knew I'd never feel for a man, had never even felt for her father, who came close.

I put the ticket in a lockbox under my bed and swore that I would never use it, that with every new and painful turn I'd remember this child, this product of marching forward, and I would let time continue to unfold.

It still sits in that box—now not under my bed, but somewhere else. I rarely think about it anymore, except when my daughter brings it up—still, even as an adult, demanding to know.

She is not a foolish woman, and yet—it has never occurred to her that maybe it remains.

After all, my dear—who would take back a night with Kennedy?

CHAPTER THIRTY-SEVEN

The doctors do their best to explain. "His heart is weak," they tell us. "This last cardiac arrest took its toll." We are—were, as it turns out—on borrowed time. We discuss the surgery. It's an option, but it's risky—due to his age and the fact that the capillaries pumping blood are very small. What has kept him alive is now a detriment to his healing.

We sit in my father's hospital room—a bright and north-facing square box that looks out over Beverly Boulevard. From up here we can see cars coming and going, entirely unaware of what is happening in these towers. A jealousy wells up in me that feels almost like rage.

Visiting hours end, and although my mom will stay, I drive back to Malibu to get more supplies. A new pillow for Dad, a change of clothes for my mom.

I pull up to 31382 Broad Beach and kill the engine. I sit with my hands tucked under me in the darkness.

I don't think about Stone down the street, and Bonnie inside. I don't think about Leo in New York. My mind is wrung out, dry. I remember nothing about the drive out here, the winding miles along the coast from the hospital.

Instead, I feel the past two months like a dream—the winding impossibility of ending up back here. All roads lead to Malibu.

The outside light switches on. Sylvia stands in the doorway—a small figure shadowed in darkness.

She makes a gesture toward me—somewhere between a wave and a beckon.

I open the car door.

"Come on, honey," she says. "Let's go inside."

I let her lead me—in the doorway, through the living room, and out to the back porch. It's not warm, not by a long shot, but neither one of us seems to care. It feels good to let the ocean breeze tear through me. I want it to carry me far away from everything this day has attached to me.

Once I'm seated, Sylvia hands me a warm patchwork blanket. Then she disappears into the kitchen, and when she returns she carries two tumblers of Scotch.

"There are occasions for the hard stuff," she says. "This is one of them."

I take my glass and tip it back. It burns on the way down.

"So," Sylvia says. "How's it going over there?"

"Terrible," I say. It feels good not to pretend. "He's . . ." I just shake my head because I can't bring myself to say it, the words. I can't bring myself to tell her what we all already know. My dad's time might be up.

"Your mother wants you to save him," she says. It's not a question.

"I can't," I tell her.

She raises her eyebrows but says nothing. She is not surprised, I realize. She already knows. Maybe Marcella has told her.

"Someday," she tells me, "I'd love to hear about it."

I set down the Scotch. "I feel like I betrayed her," I say. "Both of them."

"Did they not betray you, too?"

I look at Sylvia. She is watching me closely.

"She thinks I'm the only one who hasn't been truthful about my ticket, but she was never truthful with hers," she says. "Not really."

"Did you know?"

"Not right away." Sylvia takes another sip. The ice in the glass rattles. "She knew your father had a heart condition. She knew eventually, most likely, they would end up here. She chose to save you."

It feels like a house is being erected on my chest. I feel the pounding, the weight of wood and steal and cement.

"You didn't want her to?"

Sylvia sighs. She holds her glass between her fingers. They are long and thin with age—bony in many wrong places.

"Since you were born," she says, "I loved you. You know this. In some ways, more—although *more* is not the right word, but—I loved you easier. The love for you was easy for me. You didn't need me in the same way she did. You were your own person, and you were a force—so confident in your body, even when you were very young."

She tips the glass from side to side. I watch the amber liquid roll like waves.

"But she needed me to be something I wasn't. To live with caution, maybe even regret. She wanted me to sacrifice myself for her."

"I'm not sure that's true," I tell Sylvia now. Because I know it isn't. "I think she just wanted you."

She sets down her glass, hard. It reverberates on the side table.

"It was the sixties! There was no such thing as not sacrificing yourself for motherhood. And I refused to do it. I refused to put motherhood before my own life path."

Looking at Sylvia now, it's like I've missed this piece of her before. I've never before known her to be a mean woman, but her train of thought seems almost cruel here. For the first time in my life, I feel protective of Marcella. I feel like taking up my mother's side.

"But you had her," I say. "She was your responsibility. You made that choice, and then you didn't care."

"I cared!" Sylvia roars. "Of course I cared."

"Part of motherhood is need," I say, and as I say it I feel the need, *my* need, unhook and come loose inside me. I feel the relief at everything we've felt the past two months, at giving up, transform into a free fall. There I am, descending the well, nothing to hold on to. I plummet faster and faster. I feel breathless with this fall, with everything my body cannot and will not hold.

I pitch forward, my head in my hands. All the grief I feel, all the grief of this future, this baby, my father. The crash of reality on that cold, hard stone bottom. *Why?* I want to know. *Give me an answer.*

"There isn't one, sweetheart."

And it's not until I hear her words that I realize I've spoken the last part out loud. That I've screamed it. My prayer, my reprimand, of the heavens.

Deliver him to me.

"I wanted her to save you—selfishly, intensely—because I loved you and because the gift of the past twenty-two years would have been impossible without you. But I knew it would cost her something. I knew that she'd live timidly from that point onward.

A superpower is only super if it can regenerate. A single token is a curse as much as it's a blessing."

"But she got to save my life."

Sylvia nods. "She did. And that's why I told her about the ticket. Because that was her choice to make, not mine. Just like yours was your choice, not hers."

"I was stupid," I said. "I spent it on a guy."

Sylvia laughs. It feels out of place here.

"I came close to doing that a few times myself."

I finish my drink. I lean forward on my hands.

"Are you finally going to tell me?" I ask her. "How you spent it?"

Sylvia stands. Here, in the moonlight, her edges softened, she could be any age. She could be a child. She could be ninety-one years old.

"I'm not going to tell you," she says. "I'm going to show you."

And then she reaches inside her pocket, like she's pulling out a tissue, and hands it to me.

CHAPTER THIRTY-EIGHT

I stare at the slender piece of silver in her hands. It looks exactly like mine did, before Stone, before that night. But I know instinctively it's not. I haven't looked, I went right to New York, but I knew if I were to open that box that the ticket would be gone. The only thing from the old life that would disappear.

"You have it," I say.

Sylvia says nothing, just turns it over in her hands. The silver catches the glow of the moon and shines like a flashlight out here, illuminating her palm.

"Take it," she says.

She tosses it, like a piece of paper, and I catch it. It's light as a feather.

This is her ticket, her one do-over. She never spent it.

"Life moved only forward," she says. "I didn't want to tamper with it."

"But—"

Sylvia shakes her head. "I made my choice, and now you have to make yours." She stands. She turns to walk inside, and I stop her.

"Why?" I ask her. "Why give it to me and not Mom?"

Sylvia shrugs. She looks tired. "You're here," she says. "That's what life mostly comes down to—where you are, and when."

She walks inside. I see her pour a glass of water at the tap and then turn off the lights to the kitchen, and then she heads out to the back house.

I curl my feet underneath me and pull the blanket tighter around. The wind still whips, and the waves crash. I press the ticket into my palm.

We have the power now. We can do something about this.

I think about my father in that hospital bed, about my mother beside him. I think about all the choices that have led here, everything that was supposed to happen and did and then didn't. Everything I owe my life to.

The magic of the ticket is obvious. It is not just a chance to get it right again but the chance to save someone we love. The most powerful force on the face of the planet isn't water or wind or love. It is love directed. It is love in motion. It is life in the face of tragedy.

I sleep for a few hours on the couch, fitfully, and then, before dawn, I pack up the things Marcella requested and I get back in my car. As the sun pops up over the horizon, I feel the pain of the past twenty-four hours begin to dissolve. In another day, it will all be a distant memory, known only to me.

We can choose, I think. We can choose what story we stay in.

I turn off the 10 at La Cienega Boulevard. They've been doing construction for years and it's always jammed, but this early there isn't a car on the road save for a few pickups heading to early-morning construction jobs. I'm nearly alone.

I get there quickly, but I'm also not in a rush. I stop off for a coffee at Verve on Beverly. I pick up one for Dave and Marcella, how they like them. We have time now. We have so much of it—as much as we need.

I carry the coffees in a cardboard crate through the parking structure and two sets of elevators up to the second floor.

I shrug off my jacket and sling the overnight bag farther up my shoulder. Some of the coffee sloshes. I feel the hot pricks of liquid on my pinky finger and down my jeans. No matter. That will be gone, too.

I round the corner to room 372. I pull back the curtain.

Mom and Dad are curled up in bed. His arms are around her, and her head rests on his chest. Their eyes are closed. I watch them breathe, in and out, in and out. I slip closer toward the door. The moment feels too personal for me to be there, too intimate. I'm reminded of all the times I felt like an outsider in their love. The stolen kisses in the kitchen, the glances across the table, the Saturday nights spent sharing the same arm chair.

That was their marriage, not our family, but they felt like the same thing. They still do.

"Knock knock," I whisper.

My mom stirs.

"Honey," she says. "You're back."

She shifts off my dad, and I hand her a coffee. He wakes, too.

"This better not be decaf," he says.

"Today's oat milk latte is full force."

I lean down to kiss him on the cheek. I smell hospital, sour breath, the distant scent of urine.

I need to get us out of here.

"I have a plan," I tell them. And then, like Sylvia before me, I show them the ticket.

CHAPTER THIRTY-NINE

My mother's eyes go wide. My father squints like he can't quite make out what I'm holding.

"It's Sylvia's," I say. "She gave it to me."

Marcella gasps. My father does not shift his gaze from my hand.

"We have it now," I say.

"I can't believe this," my mother says. She is still stuck on Sylvia, on her mother, on this folded story, tucked away.

"All this time," Marcella says. "She never said anything."

"The question is just how far back we'll need to go. What did the doctor say? We can't put a stent in now but maybe ten years ago? Twelve? What do you think?" I look between them.

I see my mother blink at me and then something settles over her face. I don't want to read it, don't want to recognize it, and so I turn to my father.

His face is more set, more stoic.

"Dad," I say. "Say something."

He shakes his head. "Honey," he says. He looks to me. I see it all there, right in his eyes. "No."

"You heard me," I say. "I have this."

Dave exhales lightly. "We can't use it."

I think for a moment that they don't understand, that they think that it won't work, that the ticket is meant for Sylvia alone. "It'll work," I say. "I can feel it. You're going to die if we don't."

"Listen to her," Marcella says.

Dave and she lock eyes, and he says everything he can't out loud to her. I don't know what he is saying, but I know she understands it all. She blinks away from him, steadies herself with a breath.

"You'll do the surgery," my mother says. "It won't be fun but they've advanced the technology. It'll buy us more time."

"What?" I turn on her. "You can't be serious."

"I'm not doing the surgery," Dave says. "You heard the doctor, I'm not a good candidate."

"Dad!"

I look between them. I feel like a ghost, like I'm from the future or the past and they can't see me. Here I am, trying to change the course of history, with the *ability* to do it, but they can't hear my shouts. All they feel is a cool, unusual presence.

"What are you guys talking about?" I say. "Didn't you hear me?"

When I was little—seven or eight—I remember getting lost in the ocean. We were out at Point Dume and a big set came in, bigger than we were anticipating. Dad would always make me wear the surf leash. In the early years—before six, maybe—we'd share a board. But as I got older we'd take two out. Mine wasn't long—I still wouldn't have been able to carry it—but it was a real board. Dad always taught me the importance of the ankle leash.

"For one thing, your board can never go missing," he said. "And for another, neither can you."

Stray boards could knock a surfer unconscious, but a leash prevented a lot of foreseeable accidents. We always strapped in.

I wiped out farther in—I had caught the last wave of the set and rode it high. I turned back to Dad, hoping to see him cheering, or maybe falling off in the water near me, but he was nowhere in sight.

I paddled back out. The waves were choppy. I kept trying to ride over them at the right time, but it was hard. I had to duck under as I swam farther out.

"Dad?" I called.

No one was out there. It had been a late morning; maybe I was off from school, I don't remember. Everyone else had turned in hours ago.

I scanned the horizon—nothing. Another wave came, and as I inhaled I saw a small patch of color about five yards to my left.

The wave passed; I sputtered to the surface and started swimming hard.

Paddle, don't scream; paddle, don't scream.

I found him, knocked nearly unconscious, his board gone, getting jostled in the waves like a piece of stray clothing.

"Dad!"

I wasn't a small kid, but I wasn't a big one, either, and I couldn't lift him. I was too young. I put his arms over my board, and I held his side as I tried to swim us in.

"Come on, Dad," I said. "Hold on."

I brought him to shore that way. It was the most herculean act of strength I'd ever mustered, and have mustered since. I saved his life.

When we finally got to the sand, he was coming to. We collapsed down, side by side, the water still at our feet, licking up our legs.

I tried to catch my breath—big, heaving inhales and exhales.

I knew I had to go get Mom. I knew we had to call a doctor. But I couldn't move. All the strength I'd had I used to bring him in. I was clear out.

And then Marcella came down the beach. We were farther from our house than I'd realized—she ran at a clip. She reached us breathless. Somehow, she had known. Or, more probably: She was always watching.

"What happened?"

"Dad got knocked out," I said. I sat up. I saw that blood was running down his face from his temple. He blinked at us. Slowly. We held our breath.

And then he smiled. And I remember that smile righting the whole world. I remember that smile setting us back on our feet, back in the world.

"What's all the fuss about?" he asked. "Something happen?"

My mom shoved him. We walked back to the house—Dad limping, my arms shaking, carrying the board tucked to my side.

"You didn't wear a leash," I told him as we climbed the stairs.

"And now you see why we should," he said.

From the hospital bed Dad looks almost himself. His color is faded and he looks tired, hair flat on top. But his weight is good, his shoulders broad. It's impossible to think that something is happening inside of him that we can stop and won't. I say it to him the only way I know he'll understand, the way he has to.

"Let me put your leash on," I say. "Please."

I see his eyes soften. His hand winds out of the blankets, and he reaches for my open palm. There are wires coming out of his fingers, and his hands are cold—colder than I remember—but they warm as soon as I cover his with both of mine.

"Daddy," I say. "There's so much still ahead."

He squeezes my hand and clears his throat. Marcella turns toward the windows. I can see how much anger is still in her, how much she's struggling with.

"We can't go back," he says.

I make a move to respond, but he holds my hand tightly. *Not yet.*

"For so many reasons. We'd still end up here."

"No we wouldn't," I say. "We'd put the stent in. It could buy us a decade."

"But what about the decade we've already had?" His voice grows loud. It sounds, in this hospital room, almost booming. "I don't want to take it back. I loved that decade. I loved my life."

I look to Marcella, but her back is still to us. I see, from her reflection, that she is crying.

"We had all that time," he says. "We spent it."

"So let's spend it again."

"We can't," he says.

"Why?"

His face softens. He delivers the next part gently.

"Because," he says. "You wouldn't have Leo."

Leo. Suddenly he rushes into frame, and then he's all I can see. Our first meeting, almost five years ago on the beach in Santa Monica. Bowling on one of our early dates at Highland Park Bowl, me getting three strikes in a row, even though I hadn't bowled since childhood. Our engagement. Our wedding in Malibu. Leo cooking short ribs in the kitchen, the bungalow filling with smoke from a forgotten head of cauliflower in the oven. Director equipment all over the dining table, boxes of unfiled mail. His shoes by the door scattered like leaves.

Morning coffee and walks to Kings Road Café and his arms—wide and warm and beating with life.

Leo.

I look at my dad. And in him I see it, too. I see our first paddle out, barely three years old, eyes red with sea water. I see afternoons at school, running to his Toyota, knowing there would always be a chocolate chip cookie from Emil's. I see homework in the living room and trips to the Country Mart for fresh wax and turkey sandwiches and dinners on the deck—white wine late into the night. I see volleyball games out of state and Dad at the airport Starbucks, taking every kid's order. I see our mornings and midnights.

I see our moments like heartbeats. Next and next and next.

How can I choose? My father and my husband.

"Dad," I tell him. "I can't lose you."

From on top of the hospital blankets he squeezes my hand. "Lauren," he says. He looks into my eyes.

My dear papa, my dad.

"You never will."

CHAPTER FORTY

Lauren leaves shortly after, a mess of tears and anger. Marcella wants to take it back, too—hell, she wants to take it back just to protect her daughter from this, this devastation, what is coming—but what would it mean to take it back? Dave is right. Nothing has happened, no car accident, no sudden slip of the wheel. Just the slow and unrelenting passage of time.

After her daughter leaves, her husband seems to fold into himself, and into sleep, and once his chest is moving—up and down, up and down—she slips out, too.

She doesn't know where Lauren is, but she suspects that she won't be at home, not at the beach. She expects she is talking to her husband. Marcella likes Leo. He is not who she would have chosen for Lauren, but now that he's here—and since he has been—she knows he is right. He is foundational to Lauren in the way she has always felt she was foundational to Dave. Dave was the fun one, Marcella held the base, and she likes that her daughter will get to fly free.

She gets in her car and begins to drive. She remembers being in high school and speeding down the PCH, some Beatles song blasting. She remembers, too, the rush of hormones from her first drives out here with Dave, when they'd pull over, somewhere hidden in the bowels of Topanga Canyon, and undress each other in her back seat.

He was a good lover back then, too. He had practice—more practice than she did, to be sure. She knew he went with a lot of girls before her, but she didn't like to think about it. Not because she was jealous—she knew there were women more beautiful than her with bigger breasts and bigger appetites, but she also knew it didn't matter. Dave loved her.

No, she wasn't jealous, but instead curious. She saw these other women like portals into parts of Dave she didn't yet know. If she could have, she would have gone to lunch with every single one of them.

The sun is slipping lower as she drives out to Malibu, and with the darkening sky, she feels the edges of this moment move in closer. The gripping reality of what they are facing, trying to swallow her.

In her hands she holds Sylvia's ticket, discarded by Lauren into the folds of the hospital blankets.

Here it is now, pressed to the steering wheel, shiny and light as a feather—unbothered by the weight surrounding it.

If only, she thinks.

If only he had gone to his cardiology appointments more regularly, if only they had done more EKGs. They would have seen it sooner, wouldn't they? They could have caught it? The doctors always said he had time—but until what they never revealed—and bad on her, she never asked. She was scared to. What if they had meant death? But now she thinks: What if they had meant intervention?

She pulls up to 31382 Broad Beach Road. She barely kills the lights before she darts inside. She knows she doesn't have much time, but she also knows Sylvia will be waiting for her, and sure enough, she is.

Her mother—all ninety-one years of her—sits cross-legged on the couch. She isn't reading or watching TV. She is simply sitting. Marcella can count on one hand the number of times she has come home to her mother waiting for her, and all of them have happened after she was grown—after she was a mother herself.

"Hi, honey," Sylvia says to her. She says it softly, and Marcella feels the tenderness like cold water to the face—foreign and alarming. "Did you see Lauren?"

Marcella nods. She is having trouble speaking, trouble putting into words what she wants to say next.

"I'm sorry," Sylvia says. "I'm sorry I never told you. You must think I'm selfish."

Marcella does; she always has. Sylvia never cared how she appeared or affected anyone around her. But what Marcella feels, more than that, is sadness. That they have never had the kind of relationship that would render a confrontation like this unnecessary.

"I tried hard to have the ticket not shape my life, but it did, anyway. I was reckless and careless because everything felt ahead, everything felt like a dress rehearsal. None of it felt as real as it should have."

It's not an apology, not exactly, but Marcella listens. This is the closest her mother has ever gotten to one.

"I know you. I knew what that knowledge would do to you. I wanted you to live your life like it was the main event. I thought I could protect you."

"But you didn't," Marcella says.

"No." Sylvia shakes her head. She stands. "There is no way to protect the people we love. Eventually, life finds us. And then all we have to meet it with is grit."

"And your ticket," Marcella says.

Sylvia nods. "There is that."

"He won't let her use it," Marcella says. She comes farther into the living room. She can see her mother now, all the wrinkles that make up her face—her drooping, folded cheeks, the curtains of her eyelids. "He says he doesn't want to take back all his memories."

"And what do you think?"

Marcella doesn't hesitate. "I think that he's right."

Is it relief she sees there, on her mother's face? Or pride? She can't be sure. But there is a flicker of something, some energy past the melancholy of the moment. Something she hasn't seen in a very long time.

"She wouldn't have Leo, but beyond that—" Marcella shakes her head. "We wouldn't have the last ten years." And they have, by all accords, been the happiest of her marriage. Even better than the early years, the honeymoon years.

In these ten years, since Dave has surfed and worked less, they have fallen back into each other with a kind of ferocity that surprised her. Their marriage never floundered, no, but it was taken up with the business of life—of family, of parenthood, of bills and social obligations. There was less of that—all of that—now. And in the absence they found a robust, active, *romantic* marriage.

They made love on the weekends, Saturdays, lying in bed until eight, sometimes nine. They took long walks down the beach together and drove up the coast to Montecito, just for fun, just for lunch. But the best part was the puttering—all the tinkering and fixing and cooking and reading and scrolling that made up their together time. His presence was her balm.

She had loved it, every minute of it. She didn't want to chuck it out for something else.

"You could have them again," Sylvia says, but Marcella knows that her mother is testing her, is playing devil's advocate, something she loves to do.

"They wouldn't be the same," Marcella says, and she sees that same sentiment settle back on her mother's face.

"No," Sylvia says. "They wouldn't."

Sylvia sits. She gestures to the seat next to her, and Marcella surprises herself by following. She tucks her legs up so the edge of her knee is just grazing her mother's thigh. Her toes are cold. It's cold outside.

"I didn't save your father because I wasn't sure that if I did I'd ever have you. I couldn't guarantee it."

Marcella's breath catches in her chest, and she places her hand there, as if checking her heart. She doesn't know this. Sylvia has never told her.

"I thought he left."

"He did," Sylvia says. "He died."

Her mother looks at her, and the smallest smile curls up her lips at the edges. And then they both begin to laugh. Timid, staccato hiccups of nervous energy.

"I could see even then the way of things. And I could see that I didn't want to interfere. That's the generous telling, of course." Sylvia pauses, rubs a knee. "But it's no less true."

Marcella thinks about her grandmother in her village, saving her father. She thinks about her own mother—pregnant and alone, and then she thinks about Lauren. She thinks about the stories the women of her family have told about their roles without even speaking the narratives out loud. She thinks about everything she inherited, and everything she passed on. All the ways they got it wrong. The way they protected each other from the truth. No, from their stories about the truth.

This ticket is not a gift or a burden; it is a fact, a thing. Only in the using do we get to see right or wrong. Only in the telling, actually. She says this to her mother, now.

"It was the same ticket," Sylvia says. "For you it was a gift and a burden, and for me something to look away from. Who was right?"

"And for Lauren?" Marcella asks.

"Maybe for Lauren it doesn't have to be either."

Marcella inhales. And then she hands it to her mother. She presses it into her palm, feels the cool, soft skin there, the balm of Sylvia's touch. Familiar, if not frequent. "I don't trust myself," she says simply.

Sylvia closes both their hands around it, and for a moment Marcella is worried worried that the power of this moment, the love so evident between them, will transport them. Worried that they will inadvertently use this ticket. They could. They could go back to childhood. They could do it all again. They could see each other, really see each other. They could heal it all.

They are both feeling it, Marcella can tell. If they act now, if they agree *together*—and then the wind rattles outside, banging against the frame of a window. It startles them both slightly, but enough.

"OK," her mother says. As if that is all that needs to be said.

"OK."

CHAPTER FORTY-ONE

It's not until I'm in the car, until I hear the ringing of the phone, until his voice picks up, that I realize what I'm doing.

"Lauren," he says, his voice groggy. "Hi."

"Where are you?"

"Home," he says. "Why? How's your dad?"

"Could you meet me somewhere?"

There is a pause on the other end of the line, but I know I haven't lost him.

"Of course," he says. "Where?"

I pull into the Trancas Country Mart a little past 10:00 p.m. Stone is already parked when I get there.

I step out of the car, and he does, too. He's wearing jeans and a zip-up hoodie. His face looks tired, but he smiles, anyway.

"Hey," he says. "It's good to see you."

We take a few steps toward each other, and then he's pulling me into a hug. I melt into him. I feel the pull of our bodies together—all our history. How much has taken place, right here, between us.

"Can we talk?"

He looks behind me, as if expecting someone else, and I realize how strange this must be for him. We haven't seen each other in five years. And here I am asking him to meet me in a parking lot at 10:00 p.m.

"Of course," he says. "Let's get inside the car. It's not warm."

I hug my arms to my sides and follow him around to the passenger seat of his Bronco. He opens the door, and I hike myself up.

Once we're both inside I realize how cold I am. I rub my palms together, and Stone turns on the heat.

"Thanks."

He looks at me, searching my face.

"How is Bonnie?" I ask.

He shakes his head. "It's soon," he says. "I can't even say it out loud, I'm sorry."

I think about the last time we were here, the day she died. I close my eyes tightly and open them again.

"I was happy to hear from you," he says. "I've been thinking about you a lot. I wasn't sure if I should have reached out."

"I'm glad you called."

He turns to me. He takes my hand. "I'm glad you did, too."

I look down at our fingertips.

"Ever since I came back I can't stop thinking about us," he says. "I know this is ridiculous, I know you got married, but I keep thinking that we made a mistake. That I made a mistake."

I feel my heartbeat in my sternum, rattling my rib cage. I say nothing.

"I look at Bonnie and my dad, what they have. I want it."

"I know."

He runs his thumb back and forth against my palm. "I think we had it."

I think about the morning he left for Colorado. How I had refused to see him off, to say goodbye again. How I had stayed at my place in town until I knew he was gone, and how I didn't want to travel back to the beach for months after. How he hadn't called me, not to say he got in, not for a week, and when he did it wasn't to say he missed me, it was to tell me he wanted to surf Costa Rica and to ask if I wanted to come.

I was heartbroken, torn in two, and I remember wondering how he wasn't, how this breakup wasn't affecting him like it was me, how it was possible for him to make plans for anything at all.

All I could come up with was that it hadn't been real to him. That our decade together was just the preamble for life, for his real life, to start. That he'd look back on me the way you do on a childhood pet that had passed away—fondly and with a touch of melancholy.

This summer felt so good because it was in so many ways the answer to the question I had wondered forever: *Did he care?*

But this summer was also a fantasy. It's what happens when memory isn't muddled by more life.

I pull my hand away.

"We didn't," I say. "You remember it that way because you haven't let yourself stay somewhere with anyone else."

I think about Leo, about meeting him at the Beach Cove. Our first few dates, when getting to know him felt like watching a movie I hadn't seen in years. The familiar recognition.

"We're romanticizing what could have been, but we don't need to. We already know what was. We didn't work. And at a certain point, you have to realize that the why doesn't matter. All that matters is we didn't."

Stone nods. When I look up at him I see that he's swallowing, hard.

"Life moves only forward," I tell him, and as I say it I feel a shift down deep in my stomach. Because I know that it's true. "We can't go back," I say. "It's just not how it works."

Stone nods. "I wish we could," he says. "I'd do so many things differently. I wouldn't leave. I made too many mistakes, Laur."

I think about the idea of mistakes. The idea that there is a right and wrong way to act, to feel, to be.

"I don't know if I believe in mistakes anymore," I say. "I think there's just what we choose to do about what comes next."

He blinks at me, and I think that maybe he's going to fight me on it, or kiss me, or ask me, again, why we are here, but instead he keeps looking at me. In his face I see a thirty-eight-year-old and an eighteen-year-old. I see him at nine and twelve and twenty-five. I see every single version I have known and loved.

"What are you going to choose to do?" he asks me.

I think about my dad in the hospital, Marcella curled up against him. I think about Sylvia, standing at the front door. And Stone, right here beside me.

I take a deep breath.

"I'm going to say goodbye."

CHAPTER FORTY-TWO

I go home. Not to Malibu, no, to West Hollywood, to the place adult me lives. Our renter left early—the second season of her show was picked up and she bought a house—but still paid through the summer. The bungalow is ours again. All we have to do is collect Pea.

When I get there the driveway is scattered with leaves—debris from two months with no gardening. I take the stone path back and unlock the door.

The house is cold inside, and dark. I flip on some switches and set the heat to seventy-five. Leo and I don't fight a lot, almost never, but the one thing that we can't agree on is how warm it should be in here. Leo, even though he's always sweating, likes it balmy. For once, I agree with him.

I flip the kettle on and settle into the couch. A small cloud of dust poofs out from the couch when I sit—was anyone here? Did anyone live here this summer? Or was the renter a mirage, an idea that belongs to what seems now to be a shadow life, a shadow summer?

I sneeze once, twice, and then the kettle begins to boil.

There were times in the six and a half years I've been at this bungalow that I thought about moving. What it might feel like to be in the canyon or farther out east—Echo Park or Silver Lake, maybe. But I never considered leaving Los Angeles. It's my home. It's the place I still want to come home to. And it's the place I thought I'd raise a family.

Infertility is a dual world. There are people who cannot get pregnant who then need to turn to IVF to create their family. And there are people who can't get pregnant and then have to turn to IVF to create their family and it doesn't work. You start on the train, as hopeful as the next couple, to only realize you are headed in a very different direction.

That was us. I don't think we realized until we were a solid seven stops outside the city that we were traveling somewhere we couldn't come back from.

I pour some peppermint and lean over the counter. The tile is ice-cold—the place hasn't yet warmed up—and I slide my sweater down my arms and wrap my palms around the steaming mug.

On the counter is a photo of Leo and me. It was taken the day after our wedding: at a brunch my mom and grandmother threw at Broad Beach. We're laughing on the deck, the sun behind us. Leo is looking at me, and I'm looking at the camera. We're both wearing jeans. He has a watch of my dad's—his wedding gift—on his left wrist.

Marrying Leo never felt like a decision, it just felt like the next right thing. Our wedding day wasn't the happiest of my life because it wasn't the pinnacle of anything, it was just a continuation. Of the rightness I felt—feel—every day being with him. The assurance I get not that we were made for each other but that our futures are.

I pick up my phone. I dial his number. He answers on the second ring.

"I'm at the airport," he says.

"You're coming?"

I hear the sounds of luggage, traffic behind him. "I'm already here. Just flagging down an Uber."

I didn't even know he was in the air.

"I'm at home," I say, and I know he'll know what I mean, of course he will. And then it comes out before I can stop it, before I can even think what I'm doing, what this will mean. "There's something I really need to tell you."

A car honks. A kid screams. From somewhere far off I hear the rumble of thunder. "I'm on my way."

CHAPTER FORTY-THREE

I tell him the truth as the rain pounds against the windows.
If Leo and I are going to move forward, it will be with the full awareness of what has led us here.

"I slept with Stone," I say.

I tell him about being in Malibu and Bonnie's illness and the pull that I still have—had—to what came before. Before I was this person who could not have a baby. Before I knew what it felt like to know that everything is not ahead. That some things, even to us—Sylvia, Marcella, me—are irrevocable. I don't tell him about the ticket—it doesn't matter. It would be an excuse, now. A way to skirt responsibility. And I need to take it.

Leo is quiet, taking it in. When I'm finally finished, after I've been through the staccato beats of the summer, I can feel my heartbeat in my ears. It's not until getting it all out that I realize what I've done, what I've put on the chopping block. Everything I'm in danger of losing. My hands vibrate like hummingbirds in my lap.

Please please please please.

When I fell in love with Leo I lost a particular kind of ease. Because all of a sudden my life was sutured to someone else. If he were injured, hurt, hit by a passing vehicle, I knew my life would crumble. For the first time my happiness was so intrinsically linked to someone else that I was terrified of him even being on a plane. Anything that might take him away from me.

And now I've done the one thing that might guarantee his leaving.

"I have no idea if you'll ever forgive me," I tell him. My voice is shaking. "But God, Leo. I really hope you'll try."

He sits there, on the couch, and closes his eyes. I see the flutter of them beneath his lids. I want to put my arms around him, to take away the pain I have just caused. The selfish, stupid decision. He sinks lower. I feel the heaviness of this, of all of it, settle on my chest. The truth of the life around us.

We are not going to get pregnant. My dad is not going to miraculously recover. These are hard, impossible things, but they are also true things. And it's easier to deal with hard things when they are true. They don't float on the top of the ocean but sit, sturdy, on the sea floor. They are immovable.

Leo's eyes open, and he looks at me. I expect to see hurt in them, and I do. But I also expect to see disgust, anger—maybe even hatred. There is none of that. There is just sadness. A well of it. I can feel us both swimming in it.

"Lauren," he says finally. "I have no idea how I'll get past this."

I feel my heart begin to peel away from my chest, straining to get out. To not feel this, this absolute crushing pain.

And then he picks up my hand. Leo touches my fingers, lightly, and the graze feels like the coolest breeze on a hot summer's day. It feels like a glass of water after hours of thirst. It feels like every obvious thing about love I can think of.

It feels like being saved.

"But I want to," he says. "I really want to."

I start crying, and so is he, already, but we don't embrace. Instead we sit, side by side, our hands gripped like we're trying not to fall off a very high ledge.

"Why did you have to tell me?" he asks.

I can feel the anger, then. Not just at what I've done but that I've set it down here.

And he's right to be angry. I could have swallowed it. I took it back. I could have forgotten and moved on. Spared us this pain of this revelation. But I think about our last fertility fight. How much agency I denied him simply because it wasn't happening to his body.

"Because," I say. "You were right. I can't be the only one who gets to choose."

Leo nods, but it's bitter, resentful. It's half a head shake.

"I just want you to know how much I want this. Our family. How much I want to be here. And I think that we should—"

Leo holds up his hand, cutting me off. "I don't want to hear it," he says. "There's nothing we can do right now but this."

And he's right. There is no action to take, forward or backward, no way to take it back, no way to erase the truth that it has happened. No way to enact a future that hasn't come yet, or take us out of this present moment. All there is to do is be here, to stay in this, and to trust that one day, without knowing, it might become something else.

That's what time does, if you let it.

CHAPTER FORTY-FOUR

"Watch him on the stairs!" Marcella says. She runs to him, blocking the place where the door meets the porch. He toddles forward, and she catches him in her arms, swinging him wildly.

He learned to walk two months ago, and he hasn't stopped since. He's everywhere—on the deck—lurching toward the beach. In the living room, pulling himself up on the sofa. He only wants to be on the move.

"Got him!" she calls, more for his benefit than ours, and he peels into laugher.

My son, Damien Elliot, absolutely loves my mother.

"He takes after you," Leo tells me, which is true and funny because he doesn't actually share my genetics. We ended up using donor eggs. A young woman from Idaho with bright blue eyes and a perfect health history. I've never met her, but I know she loves to snowboard and that her favorite book is *The Statistical Probability of Love at First Sight*. That's enough for me.

It was wildly expensive—more money than I can still say out loud—but Sylvia gave it to us.

"What's money for if not this?" she said. And that was that.

We still have no idea where it came from, but we know what it's given us. Everything.

"Babe, did you pick up candles?"

Leo rounds the corner from the living room into the kitchen laden down with bags. Party supplies—barbecue chicken from Bludso's and a crudités and dip board from Ralphs. OLIPOP sodas and two bottles of red wine. The house is already decorated in streamers and white and blue balloons that Damien keeps trying to pop.

It's just us, but Leo insisted that our son's first birthday be an event.

"Counter!" I call. I refill Marcella's white wine, and she gives me a distracted kiss on the cheek. She's still got him in her arms.

"My light," she calls him, and I know that he is. I do not think I'll ever stop being grateful for the pleasure seeing my mother with my child brings me, especially after this past year, the one where we lost Sylvia.

Sylvia Ingrid Steiner passed away in September, right here at home. She knew it was coming—had known for weeks. I'd always thought she was a little magical like that. More than once I wondered if she hadn't created our tickets out of thin air, if there had even been a Hinda at all, if Sylvia wasn't, well, the witch.

We were all there with her, surrounding her bedside as she took her last breath. It was exactly how she wanted it.

"A life bravely lived," Leo said at the shiva—just us and the neighbors here at the Malibu house. It was true. No regrets.

When she began to decline she reminded me of one thing—she wanted me to know where her ticket was. Hidden in plain sight.

"It's still yours," she told me. "For whatever you wish to do with it."

Unsurprisingly, and much to our relief, Damien was not gifted one at birth. Because he was a boy or because he does not share my exact DNA, we don't know, but it felt like the breaking of something. It felt like an exhale. We've traveled so lightly in these past three years that it's sometimes hard to remember that we have changed entirely. Things are heavy until they're not.

"Lauren, have you seen my glasses?"

Dave rounds the corner, and I point to the coffee table. There they are, my father's glasses, perched on top of an open copy of his next manuscript.

He brings a hand dramatically to his forehead, and I feel, once again, the disbelief wash over me. The unbelievable reality that we are here. That he is, still.

Life does deliver miracles, as a matter of fact. The past three years are evidence of only that. One after another. The ones we chose and the ones that found us.

Dave did the surgery. It was a grueling six months, but much to the doctors' surprise, it was incredibly successful. His heart isn't perfect—not by a long shot—but he's healthy, he's *here*, and we try not to focus on the *how long* part. My father knows my son. The rest will be what it will be.

Dad goes to take one of the bags out of Leo's hand, and Leo swipes it away. "Not a chance, Pops. Have a seat. I'll get you a water."

"I'll take a beer," Dad says.

"No on that, too!"

Leo has picked up our neurosis by osmosis. I feel my heart tug once again with tenderness at this reality.

The story of Leo and I finding our way back together is grafted onto the story of us choosing donor eggs. Of us accepting the things we could not change and choosing to do it anyway. Of nights of rage and six months of living separately and a slow walk toward reconciliation. Of being done with IVF but not on the idea of a family, not really. Of choosing to do it differently.

Life isn't one thing. Neither is marriage. Horrible things happen. We do terrible things to each other. But somehow, sometimes, we are able to carry on. Maybe. And that's the magic, isn't it? Not the ticket. Not the trick of turning back the clock. Not the spontaneous, extraordinary good luck. The magic is living with it. The magic is living through it.

To stay together despite the pain. To be parents despite the shitty eggs. We are the lucky ones. We were able to make those choices.

I kiss my dad on the head and go into the kitchen. Leo is setting up the barbecue. He pulls me toward him and plants one on my lips.

Damien runs into the kitchen squealing. *Dada!*

Leo scoops him up, and Marcella starts setting up the crudités board. Dave wanders in looking to pick at the barbecue. I start to smell something burning. I remember the cake I'm baking in the oven. *Shit.*

"Everyone out!" I call.

Marcella and Dave roll their eyes, but she takes his hand, and they head outside. Leo tosses Damien over his shoulder.

I open the oven to be met with a plume of smoke. Damn it. I was hell-bent on making Damien's first birthday cake. I bought the ingredients myself yesterday, looked up the recipe for vanilla rainbow. I wanted to video him smashing it, the colorful frosting all over his face.

I take it out. It's vomiting smoke—the black clouds rising violently from this small, sad charred circle. Three extra minutes, and the whole entire thing is destroyed.

There's a moment when I think about sending Leo to Gelson's and seeing what they have in the bakery section. That thick, grocery store icing.

But then another thought crosses my mind, and before I can think whether it's good or not, it's in motion.

I lift the lid off the cookie jar—the one that has sat on the counter since Sylvia moved into this house, seventy-three years ago. The first thing she bought. A butler, holding a bottle of champagne.

It's empty, save for what I'm looking for. A small piece of metal, right at the very bottom. I look at the cake, singed black, and then I press the ticket into my palm.

This time, I'll get it right.

ACKNOWLEDGMENTS

Thank you...

To my forever partner, Erin Malone.

To David Stone, Hilary Zaitz Michael, and everyone at WME Books for their time, attention, and care.

To Kate Nintzel, Libby McGuire, Dana Trocker, Falon Kirby-Hewitt, and all the incredible people at Simon & Schuster who make my career what it is.

To my parents, my husband, my daughter, and my friends (Morgan and Hannah—first readers always), thank you for giving me endless fodder.

And to you: *Once and Again* is the first book that does not ask the question "How will it turn out?" but instead ponders: "How do I sit with what has happened?" To put it in our terms: the first post-midnight book. You, dear reader, have seen me through every stage of the wondering. For so long I wished for my life to end up exactly here. It never occurred to me that here would be the beginning.

ABOUT THE AUTHOR

Rebecca Serle is the *New York Times* bestselling author of *Once and Again*, *Expiration Dates*, *One Italian Summer*, *In Five Years*, *The Dinner List*, and the young adult novels *The Edge of Falling* and *When You Were Mine*. Serle also developed the hit TV adaptation *Famous in Love*, based on her YA series of the same name. She is a graduate of USC and the New School and lives in Los Angeles with her husband and daughter. Find out more at RebeccaSerle.com.